A BATTLE
WITH MYSELF

Chapter 1

I had the best childhood growing up. I was an average girl with a loving mother and father. I also had the best little brother I could ever ask for. I know what you're thinking. What girl in their right mind would say that about their little brother? Well Shawn and I did everything together since he was able to walk. Even before that he would sit in his little baby swing and watch television all day if I was there. I had everything a perfect family, a big loving home, and a lot of friends.

But even with all that life could give me I still felt like the odd one in the family. Well, the black sheep if you will. I was short at fourteen. I was at 5'2 and less than ninety pounds. I had long blonde hair and blue grey eyes. I also had a tan that all of my friend's would envy. I looked completely different than the rest of my family. My mother was about 5'9 and she weighed about 125lbs and in the shape of her life. She had red hair and green eyes. She really could have been a fitness model. Instead, she chose to be a crime lab analyst. She always loved science and she would always tell me that she feels accomplished at work when they find the real bad guy and bring a family justice that they deserved with the work that she did.

My father was a little over six feet tall and muscular also with red hair and green eyes. He was a professional trainer and very well known. He could help anyone loose weight and gain as much mussel as they wanted. As long as they did exactly what he told them to. There was always one person in the bunch when my dad got new clients that he knew wasn't going to follow what he said. This person nine times out of ten would complain to my father and call him no good.

I remember one time I was at my dad's gym when one of these men were there and started to yell at him. It took everything I had not to say anything even at the age of twelve I was very overprotective of my family. But then again it's not like my father couldn't take care of himself. I mean he looked like a wrestler. My father was a very calm and patient man though so he just let the man have his little rant and then escorted the man out of the building. On the way home he taught me that you can't ever blame someone else for your failures because at the end of the day the only person to blame is the one you see in the mirror.

My little brother at eight years old was almost as tall as me with red hair and green eyes as well. He was a straight A student with a bright future ahead of him. He did have some problems in school so my parents would hire a torture for him. But, as soon as we were both out of school, I would also help him with his studies. I heard him tell our mom before that he wanted to be just like me. I thought that was the cutest thing. We spent as much time together as possible. When he was really little, I would read him a bedtime story. And then when he got older to help him with his reading, he would read me a story. I was really blessed when he came into my life. I had a best friend till the end of our days. And I knew nothing would break us apart.

It wasn't just our looks that made me feel like I was the black sheep in the family it was also because I was the only creative one. I could draw or write anything. If I studied an instrument for a short time, I could just about play any musical number. I would try and teach my little brother these things that I learned in hopes that we could also do it together. But instead he was horrible at all of it. My mother would say that I was touched by a creative angel and my brother must have dogged that touch when he was born.

My parents always encouraged me to follow my passions. They would go to any concert I had. If I asked them to get me another instrument cause I wanted to learn it I would have it within a weeks' time. One year for Christmas I got more art supplies than I could ever imagine. That whole year I spent creating anything and everything I could imagine. I even started to learn the art of ceramics. I really never thought anything about the differences between my family and I a whole lot. I just thought that maybe I had taken after one of my grandparents. I wouldn't really know about them because they died before I was born. And I think it just hurt my parents to try and talk about them. So, Shawn and I learned at a young age to never ask about them.

By the time I was a sophomore in high school I was looking at a full scholarship for my ability to play the cello. I also had straight A's and the world at the palm of my hands. I still had no idea what I wanted to do with my life but I still had plenty of time to figure it out. I had even discussed taking a year off of school after I graduated high school and travel Italy for a year. I was scared to even bring it up to my parents at first because I knew of a few other people in school that wanted to do the same thing and their parents flipped. But my parents were every understanding no matter what I wanted to do. The only thing my father asked of me was to make sure to bring a friend with me and call every day. He told me if I did that then he and my mother would pay for the both of us to go. And I already knew who I wanted to bring along with me.

My best friend from school I had known since I was five years old. Her name was Jody Basher but everyone just called her JoJo. She was a tall brunette with brown eyes and a slim body like me. She was the captain of our cheerleader team. But, unlike a lot of cheerleaders that seem to be mean and pick on everyone, JoJo was a caring loving person. I think that's one of the reasons we were best friends. JoJo and I would help anyone we could. I remember one year when we held a car wash for a boy that had to have surgery and his family couldn't afford it. We almost made it to our goal and the family was very grateful for our efforts. His mother couldn't stop crying.

I had told JoJo what my father had told me about the trip to Italy and we started making plans right then and there. We even made a very well-drawn-out presentation you show her parents why they should let her go. We only got halfway threw it when they told us that they had already talked to my parents about it and if that's what we really wanted to do they would give us their blessings to go. Best thing for my parents was Mr. and Mrs. Basher wouldn't allow my parents to pay for JoJo.

So, we had our plan for after high school. And neither one of us could wait. It seemed like every time we were around each other we were planning every little detail. We had even got the area that we wanted to stay in. And knew about how much our rent was going to be every month. We still had about two years till we could make the trip but we wanted everything to be perfect down to the letter. But, then a couple of months ago she wanted to start planning our sweet sixteen. Mine was coming up sooner than hers and I told her that I really didn't want to do anything for it. Problem was I hadn't told my family that just yet,

About a week maybe a week and a half before my birthday strange things started to happen to me. I started to have these nightmares of killing my friends and family. In one dream I was standing at the foot of my parents' bed. Just standing there staring at them until they woke up. I was covered in blood. My mother freaked out jumped up to me trying to look for any wounds on my body. Trying to see where he source of the blood was coming from. I stood there staring into space not ever realizing that my father had rushed to my brothers' room in search of him.

As he rushed back to their room, he grabs me breaking me out of my trance asking me where Shawn was. My mother had already been crying as she searched my body. Tears started to form in my father's eyes as he kept shouting asking me where Shawn was. Without saying a word or looking at either of my parents. I took my father's hand and I led him to the bathroom as my mother followed us. That is where they found his lifeless body lying in the bathtub. As my mother runs to him to see if there is anything she can do to bring life back into him. My father looks at me and screams "WHAT DID YOU DO?" As he ran towards me, I held onto a knife that I had been hiding underneath a towel I had on the sink. The same knife I had used to take my brother's life.

When he was within a few feet from me I then stabbed him in the throat. He had no time to react. My father could only grab his throat and fall to the checkered floor that I seemed to hate so much. My mother who was overly distraught over the corpse of my brother didn't even notice my father fall to the floor and was slowly bleeding to death. I stood there over his body for a few more moments watching the life drain from him as he looked up at me and mouthed the word 'why'. I then walked quietly behind my mother and in a second though for me it felt like forever I grabbed her by her long red hair and slit her throat. Even though the life was draining from her body she never let go of Shawn.

She never once looked at me with the question of why in her eyes as my father did. Once the three of them were no longer breathing I proceeded to walk down the stairs into the kitchen and set it on fire. I stayed there for a short time to watch the fire grow fast and destroy everything it touched. I found myself smiling in the light of the burning kitchen. When I had my fill of watching the destruction of the place my family and I would make cookies together I started to walk back up the stairs. I went into my room and laid in my bed. I felt at peace or as if I just accomplished my one goal in life. My nightmare ended with the fire finally making its way up stairs and surrounding my bed. And as the flames grew larger covering my walls I just laid there and stared at the ceiling.

I awoke in my bed with tears falling down my face and sweat covering my sheets. I had a scream that seemed to be stuck in my throat. I was so scared that a dream like that could ever come to me that I jumped up out of bed and headed straight to Shawn's room. When I opened his bedroom door, I found him sleeping peacefully. My heart was filled with joy knowing that he was just fine. I wanted to wake him to hug him but all I could bring myself to do was thank God it was all just a dream and my little brother was safe. Then the flashbacks of my parents' death made me run to their room.

As I opened their bedroom door my father woke up and looked at me. I've always been a daddy's girl and daddy always knew when something was wrong with me. He looked up at me and saw the tears forming in my eyes. "Is everything okay sugar plum?" I looked at him and couldn't help the tears that flowed like a river from coming down my face. I tried to speak but nothing came out. Without him saying another word he moved closer to my mother and motioned for me to come climb into bed with them. I ran to him like I was five years old all over again. I wrapped my arms around him and just cried.

He let me cry for what seemed like hours as he ran his fingers through my hair. After a short time, he finally asked me "Do you want to talk about it? Was it a nightmare?". I wanted so badly but I couldn't help but wonder what he would think of me? Would he be scared or would he hate me? Would he send me to the crazy house? Would he still think of me as his sugar plum? I couldn't bear to handle what would happen if I told him. So, I answered him with the safest answer I could come out with. "No daddy not at all. I just want to be here with you". I fell asleep in my parents' bed. Next to the only man that could always make the worst thing in the world better with just a hug. The same man that I had just stabbed in my dream not too long before coming into their room. Being next to my father must have put my mind at ease because in no time I was asleep again. But this time I was in the safest place in the house. Right next to my daddy were nothing could go wrong.

I woke up when the sun started to shine through the curtains and saw that both my parents were gone. I went to my room to get my clothes for a shower. After taking a long enough shower that Shawn was yelling at me to get out, I got dressed and headed down to the kitchen. My stomach turned when I first looked at the kitchen walls that I had set fire to in my dream. But then I looked over at the table to where my family was all sitting there eating breakfast, talking, and laughing just like any other normal morning. The only thing that was different was me. Of course, my outer appearance remained the same but something inside me was different. The only problem was I couldn't for the life of me figure out what it was. I sat down with my family barely eating, running the events of my nightmare through my head. I mean I knew people could have strange dreams but this to me was way over the top. I mean how can such a happy teenager have such a horrific dream that seemed so real so life like?

I love my family more than anything. The only thing I could think of doing was hope and pray that nothing like that would ever happen again. Apparently as I sat at the table completely unaware that my mother had been trying to get my attention. My father was the one to get me out of my daze by grabbing my hand and forcing me to look at him. As I shook my head and came back to reality, he looked at me and asked "Are you okay Sugar plum? Is this about your nightmare you had last night?" I couldn't recall me telling him that I had a nightmare. Of course, then again he was daddy and daddy knew everything. Apparently, I had been thinking about all of this for a little too long cause I saw both my parents staring at me.

My mother looked over at my father and asked, "Is that why she was in our bed this morning?" Before my father could answer her, I spoke up. "Yes, mama I had a nightmare and I was afraid to stay in my room. The only safe place I could think of was in your bed." My mother went to say something but I started to speak again before she had a chance. " Before you ask, I'm fine. I understand that it was only a nightmare and I also understand that I am almost sixteen years old. And at sixteen I am too old to be climbing into bed with mommy and daddy. I'm fine and it won't happen again." My mother looked at me with a reassuring smile and said "It's okay Lilly. I just wanted to know if you wanted to do anything special for your birthday?"

Before I had a chance to answer her my father squeezed my hand again and said "Sugar plum you are never too old to climb into bed with us. Whenever you need us, we will always be here." Okay so my daddy apparently can make everything better with more than just a hug. I looked at both of them and smiled. "I know that daddy but I think that is about time that I grow up a little bit. And mom I just want a quiet night with the family. You know BBQ, games, and movie night." Without a beat to miss Shawn jumps into the conversation. "What no cake? You can't have a birthday without cake!" My parents and I all looked at each other and laughed. "Of course, cake! How could I ever forget the cake? Thank you Shawn for reminding me." I said. As my father got up he gave me a one arm hug and kissed me on my forehead "I think that sounds like a perfect sweet sixteen party Sugar plum." and he left the room to go and get ready for work. My mother gave me a wink and a smile when she got up to clear the kitchen table. And as always she made sure she left one hand free so that she could also take Shawn's game away from him. "Okay you two it's time for you to get ready for school. Lilly, remember you have that science test today. And Shawn you have that spelling test. Shawn and I looked at each other and at the same time and said "Yes mom".

As Shawn got up from the table, he ran right beside me and pulled my hair. " You little brat..." I yelled as I jumped up to chase him. I don't know if he really thought that he could outrun me or what. But man did that little kid try. I caught up to him at the top of the stars where I started to tickle him. All the memories of the first time that I got to hold him when I was eight years old. The joy that I had when we finally got to bring him home. All the nights that I woke up to him crying or climbing into my bed with me because he was scared. Singing him to sleep. All the love that I had for him. The joy that he had when he laughed came rushing through me. I was so happy that my family and I were just fine. But then Shawn screamed or at least I thought he did the images from my nightmare bombarded my mind. I went to stand up but I was too close to the edge and I fell down the stairs.

Before everything went dark, I heard Shawn crying out for our father and both of our parents calling out for my brother and I. I always thought that if you were for the lack of a better word 'knocked' out you didn't dream. I couldn't have been more wrong about that. In my dream I awoke in my bed with flames all around me. Yet, I was not on fire myself. Everything was burning around me and all I did was sit up in my bed staring at the fiery wall in front of me as though nothing was wrong.

Out of nowhere I thought that I had heard a faint knock but due to the fire the door fell to the floor. Once the ash and smoke cleared from the doorway, I saw a man. The man walked up to me and reached his hand out to me. Without hesitation I put my hand into his and stepped onto the floor. As I moved the flames around me and below me disappeared where I now was. The floor beneath my feet was cool as if it wasn't on fire just seconds ago. The man started to lead me into the hallway and down the stairs. Every step that we took the flames were no longer there. Before we got to the stairs, I looked down the hallway to where the bathroom and my family was burning to ashes. I had no idea who this man was but something deep inside me was telling me to go with him.

I had no fear, no remorse, nor regret for the slaughtering of my family. He then proceeded to lead me out of the burning house. I looked up at the man in his dark eyes and said. "They're dead, they're all dead." He spoke to me but no in a normal way. His lips never moved but it was as if he had the ability to speak with his mind. He said, "I know my child but your work is yet to be done." As soon as he said those words to me, I woke up in a hospital bed with my father by my side holding my hand.

"Daddy." I saw his eyes light up when I said that one little word. Somehow it brought peace to my heart to see daddy right there and his eyes light up when he heard me call for him. "Sugar plum you're okay. No no no don't try to sit up." As I did the opposite of what he was telling me to do. I could see the look of a father that had to deal with a stubborn teenager. "Dad I'm okay my head just hurts. What happened?" "Well honey you fell down the stairs and hit your head. You've been unconscious for a few hours now." It started coming back to me, catching Shawn at the top of the stair's him laughing and then his scream. Then the dream came back to me. I remembered the house burning all around me. I remembered the dark man who had come for me. I remembered what he said to me that my work was not done yet.

Then my father asked me a question that made my heart sink. " Who's all dead sugar plum?"

Now the only thing I saw in is eyes was worry. One of the only things I never wanted to see from his eyes. But here we were sitting in the hospital with my father's eyes full of worry. I just looked at him and put a smile on my face and said, "No one's dead daddy". "Sugar plum you said right before you woke up, They're all dead. Does this have to do with the dream that you had. If so, you know that you can always talk to daddy about anything. I told you I would always be here for you and me am." Looking into my father's eyes I knew that I couldn't lie to him. I no longer had a choice; I had to tell my father everything. So, I told him about the nightmare and about the other one when I was passed out. I was so scared I started to cry and shake. My father yet again surprised me. He jumped up and got into the bed with me and held me close. Doing everything he could to try and calm me down. "Sugar plum you could never bring harm onto our family or anyone for that matter. You are the sweetest little girl a daddy could ever ask for. Why do you think I call you sugar plum?" With that little talk daddy yet again made everything all better. I didn't even realize that my mother was standing in the doorway of my room.

I didn't know that she was in the room until she said "Lilly baby you're awake. How are you feeling?" I looked at my mother and with relief in her eye's I smiled at her. "I'm fine mommy but, I know one thing that would make me feel better." She didn't even have to ask me what it was. Well not with her words anyway. The question in her eye's asked for her. "I could use a hug from my mommy." I said to her as I reached out the arm that was not occupied from my father to her. Without hesitation my mother rushed over to my father and I and climbed into bed with us and we all held each other close. And just like that I felt like that little girl that would run to them whenever I was scared. The two people that always made me feel safe.

Looking back now I think that when I fell down the stairs my mother thought the worst. That I would never wake up again. But that's just how she was. She always thought the worst when my brother and I got hurt. And with the fact that I was unconscious to her it was like I was in a coma. A coma that I might not ever wake up from. My father had always tried to calm her down and tried to get her to come to her senses but my mother just couldn't seem to do it. My brother and I were her entire world for something to happen to either one of us would be like her life ending before it actually did. And for that reason, my father promised not to say anything to my mother about my dreams just in case she might want to send me to a shrink. And for the first time since the dreams, I let all of the negative thoughts and feelings go.

They released me from the hospital a couple of hours later. My father went off to work and my mother and I went to go get my schoolwork for the day. JoJo saw me in the hallway and I had to explain to her what had happened. "See I told you that you are the clumsiest person I know." She teased me and gave me a hug. "Tell the family I said hi and I'll see you soon." It was good to see her and I knew that I would end up spending at least an hour on the phone with her tonight. I spent the rest of the day doing my schoolwork and watching tv. Without another thought of the past 24 hours and with the exception of going to the hospital my day was going great. I couldn't wait for Shawn to get home. I still had the need to see my best friend. And yes, my little brother eight years younger than me was still my ultimate best friend.

When he got home, he ran straight to me and gave me the biggest hug. I then helped him with his homework. After his homework I got us some snacks and watched his favorite cartoons. When dinner was ready our father came in to let us know. We all sat around the table laughing and joking just like the happy family we were. I really did have the perfect life. I helped my mother with the dishes and asked everyone if they wanted to play some cards before we got ready for bed. We sat together at the same table we just ate at and played rummy for a couple of hours. After we all got ready for bed, I tucked Shawn in and he read me a chapter of Moby dick. I went to bed that night with nothing but warm feelings and the hope for a brighter tomorrow.

The next couple of days went by just as normal as could be. My birthday was tomorrow and I think Shawn was more excited about it than I was. I mean what eight-year-old can wait for cake. Mom was asking me what food I wanted and what kind of cake I wanted. She was also asking me what games and movies I wanted. The main reason I didn't want a big party was because when my mother plans something, even the smallest event, she will run around like a chicken with its head cut off. "Mom it's ok you know what my favorite foods are and what flavor cake I always ask for. I just want it to be a simple day of family fun. You really don't have to stress so much about it." She then walked up to me and put my hands into hers and with a soft kind smile she said to me "Lilly it's not every day that your baby girl your first-born turns 16 years old. In two more years, you'll be off to college and all grown up."

By the time she was done speaking she had tears in her eyes. I stood up and gave her a tight hug. Noticing that I myself had tears in my eyes due to the realization that she was right. Soon I would be out of the house and on my own. The thought of that scared me a little. "I know that I will be on my own soon. But anytime I need anything you and daddy would be the ones I call. And I know that if I ever need to come home my mommy and daddy will always have the door wide opened with open arms." She looked at me and wiped my tears away and giggled when she said "You're damn right. And don't you ever forget it."

Even though I could care less I knew that it was important to my mother so I gave her the list of all the things I wanted. She smiled as she wrote everything down like it was the best gift her child could ever get her. I looked at her in amazement hoping that the day I was in her shoes was as good of a mother to my children as she had been to Shawn and I. Looking back now, I wish that I had cherished these moments more. Because something was going to happen unknown to me and my family. In a matter of 24 hours my whole world was going to come crashing down.

Chapter 2

It was finally my birthday and I thought that I would be able to sleep in. Unfortunately, my little brother had other plans for me. He rushed into my room and jumped on my bed shouting earthquake. I wanted to kick him off the bed for waking me up but all I did was grab him by the waist and slammed him on the bed. I knew how much he hated it when I cuddled him so that's exactly what I did. I put one of my legs over both of his and held down his arms. Then I did the worst thing I could think of that would come from his own personal hell. I gave him a bunch of kisses.

"No no no no STOP IT LILITH. I'm gonna tell on you. Eeeewwww...." He started to yell. I started to do a fake evil laugh. You know like in the movies. "Ha ha ha you shall never escape my kisses! I'm the kissy monster and I kiss all the little boys that wake up their big sisters on their birthdays." He was trying to squirm out of my grasp but it was no use. I had him and he wasn't going anywhere until I let him go. I kept giving him kisses and he kept screaming for me to stop as he was also laughing. I think if I kept going he would have peed himself.

But, of course mom came to save the day. "Lilly happy sweet 16 sweetheart. Now let go of your brother. It's time that both of you come down for breakfast. Your food is getting cold and there's nothing worse than cold eggs." Boy was she right about that I have never been able to eat cold eggs. "Yes mama." Shawn and I said together as we looked at each other smiling. Then that little brat pushed me down as I was standing up and said "I'm gonna beat you to the kitchen and I'm gonna eat all of your bacon." "Oh no you don't!" I shouted back at him as I chased after him. I would have caught up to him if it wasn't for my father yelling from the bottom of the stairs "Hey could we please not have another trip to the er today?" Shawn and I stopped in our tracks and walked slowly down the stairs. We walked so slowly that our father knew what we were being smart asses. I probably didn't help that Shawn and I were giggling the whole way down.

"Alright you two stop playing around. You mother wont let me eat until you guys get down here. And I'm starving so let's get a move on here." We couldn't help but laugh as we said "Yes father." As I got to the bottom of the stairs I tried to bypass my father as I did every birthday morning. Unfortunately I didn't escape as I never did and he wrapped me in his arms for his yearly giant bear hug. "Happy birthday sugar plum. I can't believe that my little girl is already 16 years old." Then to be the smart ass that our father taught us to be he started to fake cry. "Oh my god dad it's not the end of the world. Let me go Shawn is gonna eat all the bacon." Ok ok go and have your breakfast.

I ran to the table and all my favorite breakfast food was there. We all sat down and had a great time. After breakfast daddy and I went on our annual ice fishing trip. We only went for a couple of hours but it was time that we could spend together doing what we both loved. Before we left he got a phone call. He looked concerned after he hung up. I asked him if everything was ok and all he told me was "Yes sugar plum everything is fine." But, I could tell that my father was lying to me for the first time that I knew of anyways. We left shortly after that phone call.

I could tell that this was going to be the best birthday ever. It really seemed like the best birthday when my father made a pit stop to our favorite spot. An ice cream shop called Ice Scream. We would go there all of the time the whole time I was growing up except for my birthday. Maybe daddy wanted to do something extra special for my sweet 16. I got my usual coffee flavored milkshake and daddy got his vanilla and chocolate swirl. As we headed to the house I noticed my father getting edgy. He was acting like nothing was wrong but I've known this man all of my life and there was no way he was pulling it off with me. "Daddy what is wrong? And don't tell me nothing, I know you better than that."

He just looked ahead at the road like I hadn't said a word until I said "Dad you tell me I can tell you anything. Well you can tell me anything." He looked over at me for a split second and said "Sugar plum everything is fine. There is nothing for you to worry about." I knew for a fact that he was lying. Call instincts, women's intuition, call it whatever you but, there was something wrong. "Dad I'm not a child anymore. You don't have to protect me with every little thing." By this point he could tell I was getting aggravated. I wanted to yell at him. I want to cuss at him. What is the point of becoming an adult if this is all parents will do with you to treat you like a child? It was my 16th birthday for Christ sakes and he was acting like I was Shawn's age and unable to comprehend what was going on.

"Lilith it's your birthday and I would like you to enjoy it while you still can. So please Sugar plum enjoy the ride we will be home soon." Did my father just say while I still can? What the hell was this supposed to mean? Did he mean enjoy my whole day? Or was something about to happen as soon as we got home? If I was anything like my mother then I would be trying to think of all the bad things that could have happened while we were out fishing. But, no matter what I could conger up in my mind would never have prepared me for what was about to take place. The only thing I could manage to say to my father was "Ok daddy. I'm sorry." He grabbed my hand, gave it a little squeeze and we rode the rest of the ride in silence.

I guess if this was normal for my father it wouldn't upset me as much. But, my father and I talked about everything and everything. I was raised to be opened and honest with both of my parents and them with me. Now on what my mother would call my entry into woman hood our open and honest policy seemed to go right out the window. What started out to be a great day became one of the worst. I was always told that it's bad to ask how it could get any worse. But, I asked the question to myself anyways. Looking back now I really wish I never ever thought of that question.

As we pulled into the driveway every looked as normal as it could be. I couldn't wait to spend time with my family and put this whole thing behind me. Shawn and I were going to play video games while my parents got dinner ready. I couldn't wait because I loved spending time with Shawn. So I got out of the car and I ran into the house with all the excitement in the world. "Alright Shawny boy it's time to get your butt kicked." I shouted as I ran into the house. I went straight to the living room and froze in my footsteps. Instead of finding Shawn ready to play games I found my mother on the couch crying.

I had no idea why my mother would be crying or why Shawn wasn't ready to play games and get beat by his big sister as he always did unless I let him win. And that was only a couple of times because I didn't want him to think for a second that he was better than me. But, yet on my 16th birthday he was nowhere to be found. And my mother was on the couch crying and I do believe my father was still in the car.

I walked up to my mother. Afraid of how to approach her. I swallowed my fears and simply asked her "Mommy what wrong? And please don't tell me everything's ok cause daddy already said that to me. But, I should know better you sitting here crying and daddy is still in the car. We have always had an understanding of honesty. But now,

I'm being shown differently. Please Mommy tell me the truth. And for the love of god please please tell me where Shawn is." I knew at this point in time neither one of my parents could tell me that nothing was wrong.

My father had finally come into the house and to the living room to where my mother and I were at. He put his hand on my shoulder and asked me to have a seat. I sat next to my mother on the couch while my father sat in his chair. I couldn't help but think that every father had his own chair. We sat there in silence for what seemed like forever to me. When my father finally spoke the words he said made my heart drop. "You know that we love you and your brother more than anything in this world right?" Isn't that what a parent says to a child when they have bad news. Is that why my father told me to enjoy my day while I still could. All I could say was "Of course I know that daddy." Even though there was fear in my voice I tried my hardest to stay strong. How else was I supposed to answer that question anyways?

As we sat there and continued in silence I could no longer take it. "Can one of you please tell me why you're being so strange and for the love of god tell me what the hell is going on!" My mother had started to compose herself but with my outburst I guess it was just too much for her to handle. She started to cry again. My father looked at me not with disappointment but with the look of regret mother tried to say something but she couldn't. The tension between the three of us was building with every second.

I couldn't take it anymore. "Mom dad what is going on. apparently there is something you have to tell me and you don't want to. Is it Shawn? Did something happen to him?" I hadn't realized it but by the time I got all of that out I had pushed my mother back. I had jumped up and I was on my feet yelling and crying. My father got up and wrapped me in his arms and calmed me down enough to where I could sit down and listen to what they had to say. I had never in my life been so scared and so frustrated. My father put his hand on my knee and started to tell me what I guess would be the hardest thing he would ever have to say.

"First off Shawn is fine. Your mom sent him to a friend's house. Now I was scared, frustrated, and confused. Why would my mother send him to a friend's house knowing that we were supposed to spend the day together? But, what my father had to say next was so much worse than anything anyone could ever say to their child. I know now and knew back then that it was never to hurt me. But, to keep the open and honesty agreement in place.

"When your mom and I got married we wanted nothing more than to have a child. We tried for many years. We went to doctors and specialists to try and find out why we hadn't had any luck." My father moved his hand from my knee to my hand and squeezed it a little harder. The more he spoke the tighter he squeezed my hand. And the more he spoke the worse my stomach sank.

I wanted him to get to the point but the more he spoke the more scared I was of how this conversation was going to end. "Well after a long time of your mother and I trying we found out that it was almost impossible for me to have children. So we did the only thing that we could do. " I interrupted my father as I looked into his eyes and said "What are you trying to tell me that I'm..... I'm adopted?".

My mother who I completely forgot was sitting beside me finally spoke up. "Yes sweetheart we adopted you when you were a month old. When we brought you home we were the happiest we had ever been. You were every bit of perfect. You were so beautiful and smart we decided that we wouldn't tell you about the adoption until we absolutely had to." She tried to continue but I couldn't listen any more. I jumped up and screamed at both of them.

"WHAT THE HELL!!! You thought that on my 16th birthday you just had to tell me that I'm not your real daughter? Why today of all days would you tell me that." I didn't even give them a chance to answer. I couldn't take it anymore. I started to leave when both my parents tried to speak to me at the same time. But, I wasn't about to hear anything else they had to say. "Just stop it! I can't listen to this anymore. I don't have to."

Before they could say anything else I ran out the door. I had no Idea where I was going to go but I couldn't stay in that house anymore. Not with the people who have lied to me my whole life. I just ran down the street. I kept running and running. I ended up at our city park where I saw the swings were free. I was a little tired from running so I decided to stop and sit on one of the swings. I just sat there wanting to cry but yet I couldn't bring a tear to my eyes. I wanted to know why they felt as if they had to tell me today of all days. Why would they want to destroy my sweet 16 after just a couple of days ago they were saying how it had to be perfect? What were they thinking? Was this there a way of saying that deep down they hated me?

But, if that was the cause why would they have kept me? Was Shawn adopted as well? My father said that it was almost impossible to have a child not completely impossible. And I remembered my mother was pregnant with Shawn. But, then again they lied about them being my parents. And I remember seeing something on tv where women were acting like they were pregnant and fooled their whole families. Could my mother really have done all that. And if so why would she wait eight years to adopt again? I didn't know what was the truth and what was a lie anymore. My head was spinning with questions. My whole life was a lie. How could I trust them anymore?

Then the most important question came to me. If my mother and father were not really my parents then who was? What were they like? Why did they give me away? All questions I wanted to ask. All questions that I needed answers to. Would my fake parents even know who they were and would they help me find them if I wanted to meet them? Of course I wanted to. How could I not? I knew that I wouldn't be able to get any of my questions answered sitting here on this swing. And yet I couldn't bring myself to start walking home. I couldn't even bring myself to stand up. It was like my mind was trying to tell my body what to do and yet my body was doing whatever it wanted to which was nothing. I just needed a little bit longer to calm myself down.

Looking back I could never remember being this upset this heart broke. I wanted the tears to fall down my cheeks but yet they wouldn't fall. I wanted to go home and go straight to my room but I knew my parents would be shortly behind me. My plan was to stay here and wait until enough anger passed through me. Just enough so that I could face my parents with whatever they wanted to discuss with me. And hopefully they would be able to answer the questions that I had for them. They owed me that at least. As I was planning on going home my father showed up. Apparently he was behind me . I didn't know that he was there until he sat on the swing next to me.

"Hey Sugar plum. You want a ride home? or do you just want to stay here?" I didn't want to talk just yet. But, he was my daddy after all. Without looking at him I softly said "I want to go home please." We got off the swings and headed to the car. He tried to put his hand on my shoulder while we were walking but I just brushed it off. Yes no matter what he will always be my father. Just at this point in time I was still so mad at him and my mother I didn't want his comfort. I know that in a way it was breaking his heart but to me I wanted him to hurt as much as I was.

We got into the car and rode the whole way home in silence. I knew that when we got home that's when my parents would want to sit down and talk about everything and at this point even with me wanting answers I still wasn't ready yet. But, then again would I ever truly be ready to have this conversation. I had to face this head on. My parents always taught me to be strong and on the day I needed to be the strongest I ended up being the weakest I have ever been.

My father kept looking like he wanted to say something but never did. We got home and I just sat there in the car looking at the house I grew up in. Trying to wrap the past few hours in my head. My father walked over to the passenger side and opened my door. "You coming in Sugar plum? Your mom and I really would like to explain everything to you." I just nodded my head and slowly got out of the car. As we got closer to the door a million things went through my mind. For instance what exactly was going to be said. What inspired them to tell me on my 16th birthday after making plans of celebrating? Where are they going to tell me Shawn was adopted? Where are they going to tell me my real parents wanted to meet me?

Did they want me to leave and never come back? Well if that was the case my father wouldn't have come out looking for me would he? I didn't know how the rest of my day would go. And to be honest I really didn't want to know. I wanted to go back to last night and wake up again and have the day I was supposed to have. Standing at the door I knew there was no going back. I knew I couldn't turn around and run no matter what. I had to face this head on. Grab the bull by the horns as my father would say.

And just before I walked through the front door I realized my father and I had a stronger relationship than my mother and I. Me and him did everything together. While Shawn and my mother did their own thing. I had been lost in my own thoughts so deeply I didn't even realize that my father had opened the door and my mother was standing there before me. She appeared as though she wanted to hug me but thought better of it to give me my space. But, then again space wasn't what I needed.

I needed clarity, peace of mind, for Christ sake I needed this all to be a bad dream. And yet it wasn't. It had become my reality. I knew I had to be strong for my parents. They both looked as if years had been taken away from them within a few hours. They both taught me to be stronger than your average person. Maybe to prepare me for the day that they finally told me the truth. I walked inside and gave my mother what she so desperately needed. A big loving hug from her little girl. My father wrapped his arms around my mother and I and the three of us just stood there in a warm embrace.

When the hug finally broke My mother and I were holding hands and we all just stood there like in a moment of silence. It seemed as if no one would break this moment and I just couldn't take it any longer. And as I was about to break the silence my mother surprised me by speaking first. "Come on into the living room sweetheart. There is much that your father and I need to discuss with you." I was no longer hesitant, I needed to know everything. I followed my parents to the living room to finally find out the truth. As we sat down I could see my father with worry in his eyes and my mother with tears in hers.

The tension between the three of us was unbearable. Nothing that I had ever felt before. It seemed as if they just wanted to stay in this moment forever without ever saying another word. The longer we sat there without words being exchanged the more the pit in my stomach worsened. I couldn't take it any longer. If they weren't going to speak first I had no choice but to. The pit grew more when I tried to speak. I knew my mouth was opened but yet the words themselves could not escape. And even though my parents could see me struggling they themselves couldn't speak. To this day I couldn't tell you if I had finally grown the strength to speak or the pit of my stomach finally burst. But, I broke the silence. It's like I couldn't take it anymore and something in me just snapped.

"I could think of a thousand questions to ask you maybe even a million. But, there is only one that deep inside me must have answered. Why.... why today of all days would you finally after 16 years would you tell me what you told me? Why in the world could this not wait until tomorrow or why did it ever have to be said? You both will always be my parents. So why why did you even have to tell me?" It seemed like an eternity until my father spoke up to finally answer my question. "The reason we haven't told you until today is because we never thought we would have to. Well until today that is. There are things about your birth parents that might affect your very close future and we didn't want anyone else to tell you."

What did that mean by that? Who else knows about my adoption? And why how could it affect my near future? "Okay okay just stop a second. It's like you're trying to tell me little by little. Why can't you just come out with it?" "It's harder to explain than it seems it should be sweetheart. You hail from different kinds of people. And I mean very different." My mother said to me as she tried her hardest to explain what my father had said. The more words she said the more tears would fall from her eyes.

I tried to sit there and understand what my mother was saying. My real parents were different? Well no kidding they were different, everyone is different in their own way. Now I started to get scared. I didn't know anything about adoption. But, I mean wouldn't this only affect me if they were trying to get me back. I was adopted though and they couldn't actually do that right? With me being 16 wouldn't I have a say in who I was going to live with. "So what you're saying is that my real parents are going to show up and take me away from you? I mean until you tell me everything that's what it seems like you're trying to say to me." I said to them with terror in my eyes.

That's when my father stood up from his chair and sat on the other side of me and both my parents held me in their arms as my father once again spoke to me. "No no no Sugarplum when parents adopt their child that child stays with them forever. No one is going to come and take you away from us. Not now not ever. The reason why our explanation is so hard is because your real parents are very very bad people. We worry about you second guessing who you really are after hearing about them."

What did my father mean when he said bad people? I couldn't take it any longer. It was as if they were trying to give me a bunch of riddles that I couldn't figure out. How hard was it to tell me the truth? Why would I ever second guess who I was? I'm the splitting image of my father. He raised me and we both where now the same. My emotions finally got the best of me. "Mom Dad stop with the bullshit! What is so important about my real parents and how would someone else tell me before you? You do realize that every word you speak you're freaking me out more and more. Oh and if it was so important to tell me today then why dad why were you both just fine this morning? And why isn't Shawn here? What the hell is going on?"

I sat down on the coffee table waiting for them to tell me. Apparently all that yelling took a lot out of me because I was having a hard time catching my breath. My mother just sat there crying too much to speak. For a woman who taught her daughter to be so strong she was acting very weak. My father looked shocked word he grabbed the tv remote and turned it on. Of course without my brother or I eating it the tv was on the news. I was astonished. Did my father try to block out all of my questions by simply turning the television on? Did he really think that I was that naive to where I would see a flickering screen and forget about everything that had gone on throughout the day? That is until he shut the tv off again and I could recollect my thoughts and him and my mother had time to figure out the answers to the questions that they could? It didn't make any sense to me my father knew I was smarter than that.

But then I heard something that caught my attention and I had no choice but to turn around and watch. It was the breaking news. Not only was it breaking news it was news from another state. As the announcer talked all of my attention was glued to the tv and towards the end I had nothing but fear coursing through my body. "Breaking news from Mississippi state correctional facilities Mr. and Mrs. Smith 16 year residents have broken out. How these criminals with no communication known to the warden and escape two prisons on the same day are still under investigation. Their destination is still unknown. If you see or hear anything about Frank or Susan Smith please contact your local authorities. Please keep in mind these two are very dangerous. If you heard about their cause they killed 12 people in a 24 hour period on Halloween almost 17 years ago. Please do not open your doors or try to apprehend them ourselves."

Then when their pictures showed on the screen it was almost as if I was stabbed in the heart. The woman that they showed looked just like me just 20 years from now. The blonde hair blue eyes. Same facial features. The man had hazel eyes and brown hair but was just a little darker than me. I mean if anyone would see the three of us together they would automatically assume we were a family. But, we couldn't because these people were crazy. Before I could try my hardest to make sense of what was going on the reporter continued with "They both however left a note stating that there little girl was finally turning 16 years old today and it was time for them to show her the way." At that moment it didn't matter what else the reporter had to say. My heart dropped. I couldn't speak nor could I ask either one of my parents for an explanation. I just sat there frozen. I knew my parents were trying to give me a few minutes to try and comprehend what they were or should I say the news was telling me. "So what you're trying to tell me is that my real parents are killers and now they are out of prison looking for me?"

Everything stopped around me and my head was spinning. How could this be? My mother started to cry even more than before. My father on the other hand stayed strong and put my hand into his as he simply said "Yes Sugar plum. All of that is true." He squeezed my hand even tighter as he continued on with his explanation. "We... your mother and I never wanted to let you know who they were unless it was extremely important. With the news of their escape your mother and I thought it was in your best interest to know the truth. But, you must know we never ever wanted you to find out on your birthday. And your adoption records were sealed. But, we can possibly know the extent of their intelligence. Nor can we know for a fact their contacts. We didn't want someone to show up at the door and you find out that way."

My mind was spinning. I didn't know what to make of all of this. My parents must've lost their minds. None of this could be real. They have got to be messing with me to surprise me with an ultimate party right? I started to look around our family home looking for Shawn and my friends to pop out of somewhere. But, as I looked around no one came out. And as I looked at my parents it started to sink in that this is now my reality. "Okay so I come from murderous parents. I'm doing my best to understand that. I mean you can't just expect me to take in this information and be good with it. However I am doing my best to do it." What surprised both my father and myself was that my mother who had been quiet other than her crying finally spoke to me.

" Sweetheart, we were not saying you had to comprehend all of this information all at once. We just finally had to let you know because we don't know what will happen in the near future." In the near future? What the hell did they mean by that? How could my crazy birth parents have any effect on me if I've been adopted? I had no idea how to even come close to process what was going on. The room seemed to start spinning out of control. Shortly after everything just went dark. I guess fainting after having to take in so much traumatizing news is a normal thing. Right?

I woke up shortly after, still a little dizzy and disoriented so both my parents told me to go to bed. I did as they told me not because I was always supposed to listen to them but because honestly I could stand to be around them at the moment. I sat up in my room with only my thoughts. Trying to understand everything that had taken place. Thinking that maybe if I had asked for a big birthday party maybe just maybe I wouldn't have found out today. But, then again would it have really made a difference which day I would have found out. I don't think that would have made the pain any less than what I was feeling now. I mean how could my parents keep that from me for so long? Are they going to feel different about me now that I know the truth? And what about poor Shawn, how is he going to take the news?

While I was thinking about the million and one things going through my mind my cell phone rang. It was JoJo calling me. I didn't really want to answer it but, then again I needed someone to talk to. I decided to answer the phone all though I wasn't sure that I was going to tell her the events that happened today. "HAPPY BIRTHDAY GIRL!!!" She screamed into the phone as she always did on my birthday. "Thanks JoJo. How's your day?" I asked her. I guess my tone was a bit down cause right away she could tell that there was something wrong. Because she asked me "Okay girly what's wrong? You should be so happy today. I mean you did choose to spend your birthday with your family without me but you know I'm not upset about it." She said sarcastically.

This made me laugh a little bit. But, I still didn't say a word. I found it almost impossible to speak without tears forming. I could tell that JoJo was starting to worry. I never went this long without saying anything to her. And I think she could also hear the pain in my small laugh I had just given her. She was my best friend and I still found it impossible to tell her what was going on. In that moment I figured out why my parents told me the way that they did. It was because it was way too painful to just say it out right. So I did it their way "Have you watched the news today by chance." I managed to ask her. "Ewww no. You know we have a couple more years before we have to keep up to date with the crazy in the world." That's what we would always tell each other growing up. The news was something we wouldn't worry about until we turned eighteen. "JoJo listen I need you to turn the tv onto the news and let me know when you see the Smith's."

I knew that she wouldn't question me about it. We've always had that relationship of don't ask questions just do what you're asked. We just stayed on the phone in silence until she finally said ""Here it is. Wow those people are nuts." "Yeah they are." was all that I could reply." We stayed on the phone without speaking a word while she finished listening to the reporter. I knew when she heard the part of their letter saying that their daughter just turned 16 today because she said "Holy shit dude that's crazy their kid has the same birthday as you Lilly that's so trippy." I knew that she wouldn't be able to figure it out by herself but, that didn't stop me from shaking my head when she said that.

A few moments later she came out with "Oh my god Lilly you look like both of them. You don't think that…… that you're related to them do you?" I was in shock that she actually started to put everything together. I mean I loved JoJo but she wasn't the smartest person in the world. "Those are my real parents Jo." I said to her. She didn't say anything for a while so I had to check the phone to make sure the call didn't drop. It didn't I just think that she didn't know what to say just as I didn't when I found out. "Wait a minute this is a joke right. I've known you forever there's no way that you're adopted." If this was going to be the same when we told Shawn I didn't want him to ever know. I mean it has to be harder to tell your brother than your best friend.

"No JoJo this isn't a joke. They are my real parents my mom and dad told me today. The same way I just told you actually." "But, why would they tell you today? I mean come on of all days today is the day they choose to do it?" And then the question of how this would change my near future came back to me again. I had tried so hard to put that in the back of my mind. But, leave it to JoJo to think the same way as me. "I guess they wanted to tell me because they escaped today and with the letter I'm thinking they're a little worried that it might impact me if anyone finds out who I really am." That was the only reason I could think of. I mean it did make sense people could look at me differently right?

But, JoJo thought of something else, something much worse. "What if the Smith's are actually looking for you and find you? I mean that is what the notes said right? What are the chances of them finding you?" This made my heart drop. What if they did find me. Would my family be safe? Who was I kidding they're crazy people no one in the house would be safe if they did find me. But, how would they do it. I was adopted in a closed adoption. "Well you know how the internet is nowadays and who's not to say that they gave the Smith's your parents' names when they adopted you? Did you ask your mom and dad that?" My head started to spin again. All these questions that I didn't even think of asking. What did it mean to have a closed adoption? Would they be able to find me? What would they do if they did? This started to become more and more for me to handle.

"Lilly are you there? Please tell me your ok. Oh my god did I say something that I shouldn't have? Oh I did look I'm so sorry nothing like that will happen. These people seem way to dumb to be able to find you like that." I knew that she was trying to help me but, she was actually making everything worse. Manly because now I had to get more answers from my parents to make sure everyone in the house was safe. I wasn't ready to talk to them about this just yet but, I felt as if I had no choice in the matter. "JoJo calm down I think I'm the one that should be flipping out right now. You didn't make anything worse. You just had me realize that I really need to go talk to my mom and dad about this and not hold it off any more. Plus they may think that I don't love them anymore if I just keep myself in my room. I'll call you later love ya girly." I could hear the relief in her voice when she replied back "Ok love you to girly and remember you can call me any time." I hung the phone up right after, wiped the tears from my eyes and started to go down stairs to talk to my parents.

"What did we do? We could have just given her today and told her tomorrow. Now this is how she is always going to remember her sweet sixteen. We have to be the worst parents in the world." I heard my mother saying to my father. It killed me to hear her cry and for her to think that she's a bad mother because they told me the truth today was nuts. My parents are the best parents that I could ever ask for. And if you really thought about it I was the lucky one for having them as my mom and dad because of all the children they could have chosen they chose me.

My father was starting to talk right as I was going to walk up to them. "We knew that this day could happen when we adopted her. She would never think that about you not for a second. She knows that we love her and she loves us. The thing is that she needs time to let all of this sink in. She'll come down here if not tonight but tomorrow and we will all sit down and talk about this. And you know what's going to happen after we all talk?' My mother said in the saddest voice "No I don't know. What will happen?" I could hear the smile in my father's voice as he told her "We will end the conversation in a group hug like we always do when it's a hard conversation. Because she knows how much we love her. And just to make sure you know that she knows we will remind her of that fact."

He was right that was how it would end because it always did. And I did know how much they loved me. They wouldn't be this upset if they didn't. "I don't know Berry. This just seems like too much for her to handle especially on her birthday. I even made it seem like the biggest deal in the world than we did this to her. How can we ever make up for that?" I couldn't listen to it any more. I wanted my mother to know she was the best and not let her think for one more second that she was the worst.

"Mommy? Daddy?" Was all I could manage to say as I ran up to them and hugged them both. Okay my father wasn't one hundred percent correct of how this conversation was going to go. But, I just couldn't help myself. I wanted to hold them close. We stayed in that embrace for a few minutes. Before the three of us let go I said to both of them "guys are the best parents I could ever ask for. I'm not mad at you for telling me on my birthday. I love you both with all my heart." We all pulled back and I sat down in the middle of them on the couch. I didn't want them to try and explain any further. There was only one thing that I wanted to know. "Are we safe? I mean they did get out of prison so they have to be somewhat smart right? Will they be able to find us?"

My mother looked shocked by my questions. My father on the other hand didn't seem fazed at all. She looked at my father then looked over at me. She still had tears in her eyes. I could see the pain that she was feeling at that time. My father put my hand into his and said "No sugar plum they won't be able to find us at all. We moved far away and changed your name. You were born Ann Lee Smith. The courts sealed your records so that in the event that they ever got out you would be safe." I looked at him and he didn't seem to have a worry in the world. But., then I looked over at my mother who seemed to be very worried but tried her hardest to hide it.

"Mom what's wrong, what are you not telling me?" I asked her. All I wanted was the truth. And in my defense I don't think I was asking for a whole lot. "It will always be a worry while they're out that they might find you. The possibility is slim to none but I worry about it myself. Just remember we have your father so we're safe." Apparently this upset my father because he had something to say to my mother right after she finished. "JOY.... Why in the world would you say something like that? They are not going to find us at all. You talked to the attorney this morning and he said that everything was sealed shut. So why Joy why would you ever put that into her head?" My father was furious at this point. I don't think I had ever seen him this mad before. I knew what my mother was trying to do. She was trying not to lie to me. My father was also trying to protect me.

"Mom, dad stop please. I understand I'm safe. And that nothing will happen. I just want to go back the way that things were before you told me anything. So can we please get Shawn back home and have the family night that we were supposed to have? Or are we going to let this mess up the rest of the day?" I just wanted to stop talking about it today. My parents were fighting which they never did. Shawn wasn't here on my birthday. Not to mention every time we started to talk about them I started to get a headache. The only thing I could do was try my hardest to try and get the family back on track like nothing ever happened.

"Shawn's next door if you want to go get him then your father will start the grill and I'll get the games out of the closet." My mother said. Before I left I gave both my parents a big hug and told them that I didn't want my little brother to know anything about this. They both agreed to it and sent me to go and get my little brother. When I stepped out of the house I felt a wave of relief. I wanted nothing more than to stop with that conversation. I was hoping that my parents were finally at ease. Yet again I knew that they wouldn't be not until the Smith's were captured. As soon as I knocked on the door Max the neighbors son answered the door and let Shawn know that I was at the door. He came out and gave me a big hug and told me happy birthday again. "Thanks, you little brat. Let's get home and start the party. What do you say?" He smacked me on my arm and said "Race ya!!" And with that we were both running towards the house.

We both got to the door at the same time and fought to be the first one in the house. Mom walked to the door to see us trying to get through at the same time. I thought for sure she was going to say something to us but instead she just shook her head and walked back into the kitchen. I had to do the only move I had to get in first. I tickled Shawn's side and he jumped backwards and I had my victory.

I could smell the food on the grill as soon as I stepped into the house. Shawn ran up behind me and shouted "THAT WASN'T FAIR!!!" "Life's not fair butt head." We were both told to get to the picnic table and we did as we were told. As we all sat down I looked around at my family with more admiration than ever before. We then played games and watched movies until about two in the morning. It was better than I ever thought it could be.

My dad was going to carry Shawn into bed but I had already put a blanket over him and told my father that we should just let him sleep down here for a night. The three of us went up stairs and went to bed. Of course my parents tucked me in like I was a little girl, a gesture that I will always cherish. I wish I could go back to that night. The events that took place after that will hunt me for the rest of my life.

Chapter 3

I went to bed with the thought of everything that had taken place today. How could any of this be my life? How could I have been created by those monsters? I have read articles of serial killers a little bit but to have their blood running through my vein's. Would I become one someday? I didn't understand how that would work. And not knowing was the scariest part of it. But who would know me better than me right? I would never be capable of such a heinous act to anyone. And then I started to think about my dreams. Me killing my whole family and the strange man telling me my jobs not done. All of this before I even found out about my birth parents. Was it all just a coincidence? It had to have been most killers have thoughts about it all their lives. I'm sixteen and I only had a couple of those dreams. I never even thought about it when I was awake. "Oh my god I'm over thinking everything just like I always do." I said to myself. I always over think on everything. "Wow I must really be like my mom." That thought right there put my mind at ease. My mother and father might not be my blood but, I am just like them. And I was proud of that fact. I laid down and slowly drifted off to fall sleep.

I awoke to a loud bang downstairs. I looked at the clock and saw that it was only two o'clock in the morning. I thought that it was Shawn trying to get something to drink and just rolled my eyes and rolled over to try and go back to sleep. As soon as I closed my eyes, I heard it again. "Oh my god Shawn why would you want to wake up the whole house at two o'clock?" I asked even though I knew there was no way he could hear me. I decided to go downstairs and help him with whatever he was doing and yell at him for waking me up so early. As I stood up, I heard another bang. This one softer than the last two. What the hell was he doing this early? I opened up my bedroom door and saw the light to the dinning room on. Ok something was definitely wrong with that. Why would he be in the dinning room and not the kitchen? That's when I heard a soft whimper and thought that Shawn had hurt himself. I started to run down the stairs and to the dinning room. But when I got there I froze. I couldn't move a muscle. The only thing I could do was give a low cry as I whispered "Daddy?"

What I saw I couldn't even comprehend. My whole family was tied to the chairs of our dinning room table and my father was unconscious. Shawn was crying and my mother was trying to say something, but all their mouths had been taped. I saw my mothers' eyes going from me to the place she kept our China and then back to me. I thought she wanted me to get Shawn out of the chair because he was sitting right in front of it.

I went to go get him and that's when I heard a voice that sent chills down my spine. "Oh, Darling look at our little Ann. She's just as beautiful as she was on the day that she was born wouldn't you say so." It was them. I have never heard their voices before and they where in the shadows so I couldn't see there faces but I knew it was them. They had found me and now because of me my family was in trouble. They stepped out from the shadows to where I could see them. They had smiles on their faces like something out of a horror movie. I put my hand in my pocket to get my cell phone so that I could call for help until I realized it was still on the charger in my room. I looked at my family and then back at these monsters trying to figure out what they wanted. Then it hit me. They wanted me. They wanted to show me the way just like they said in the letter that I saw on the news. There was only one thing I could think of doing and that was to play dumb.

"Um, ma'am my name isn't Ann it's Lilith I think you're in the wrong house." My voice was so shaky I could barely get out the words I was saying. They both looked at each other and gave a small chuckle. "Ann it's not good to lie to your parents. We've been watching you all day and we saw when you watched the news. We even followed you to the park." He said. His voice was deep and raspy. "Again, I don't know who you are." I tried to keep playing dumb but the look in the faces showed that they knew better. "Don't lie to your father Ann. I'm sure you were raised better than that. Show him the respect that he deserves." Her voice was very soft like a little girl but yet it was firm like a mother. I knew that I should keep my cool and be afraid but something in me snapped. I didn't like them calling themselves my parents. They weren't my parents. My parents and my little brother were tied to a damn chair. And these monsters were trying to claim my parents' places. That was something I could not let happen.

"You are not my parents and he doesn't deserve and damn respect. You break into my home and tie my family up. Three people that have never done anything to you and you want me to show you respect? Are you out of your freaking minds?" They both just stood there staring at me like I was the crazy one. Then he took two steps towards me. I could see the fire in his eyes. He was infuriated with my insubordination and I didn't care. Something in me made it to where I wasn't afraid of him. My father could scare me but this man in front of me couldn't. "You better not ever take that tone with me or your mother again. Or I'll....." I cut him off before he could finish his sentence. "Or you'll do what bend me over your knee. I'm sorry but you are not my dad a dad is one that takes care of you. That tucks you into bed and makes sure you know how to throw a ball. He takes you to ballet and then sits through all your performance's. You may have been the one to help bring me into this world but that sure as hell doesn't make you my dad." I found myself yelling at the end. I had no idea what had come over me.

Before I knew it, Frank had run up to me pulled my hair and slammed me down to the ground. It hurt but I barley felt it. I don't know if it was the adrenalin rush or if he wasn't as strong as he looked but I knew that if I wanted to save my family, I was going to have to obey these crazy ass people. So I decided to play along with them. "I'm sorry dad I shouldn't have spoke out of line it wont happen again. Just please leave them alone take me away but don't hurt them there good people." Susan came up to us and put her hand on Franks "Sweetheart we can not blame her for how she thinks. She has been brain washed her whole life we just have to have patience with her and show her the right way." Her words made me quiver with fear. What did she mean when she said show me the way? The way of what? And how could I be brain washed when I was raised by two other people and didn't spend a second with them? I had nothing but fear and confusion at this point. But I also knew I wanted my family to survive this horrible night.

Frank looked at Susan and let them go. I wanted to cry but that would show them that I was afraid of them. And if you're afraid of someone then you can not trust them and that is something, I couldn't let them think. I needed them to believe that I trusted them, and I wanted to learn from them. I didn't care what I had to do as long as they didn't hurt my family. I looked over at Shawn and he was crying. With every tear that fell from his eyes my heart shattered more and more. It made it even more difficult not to cry seeing him like this. My mother was looking at me with love but also with fear. I wanted my father to wake up so I would truly know what to do. My father and I never needed words just a glance and I knew what he wanted to do. But to my dismay he was still unconscious with blood running down his forehead where they had hit him. I had never seen him so venerable so helpless. I needed to be the strength of my family. Hopefully just for a little while longer. But how was I going to keep them all safe from these crazy people?

I asked the only thing I could think of asking to them "So you're here to bring me home then? And we can be the family we were all deprived all these years." They looked at me with appreciation in their eyes. Susan even had a tear fall down here cheek. I was trying to do everything that I could do to get them out of the house. If I could get the three of us to leave them my family would be safe. Frank looked at me and said, "Not in that order but yes." My heart dropped I could barely breathe because I knew exactly what he meant. They were going to show me the way by making me watch them kill my family. I looked at all three of them one by one. When I got to my dad, I saw that he was finally coming to. I could feel the tears forming in my eyes. But I couldn't let them fall. I had to stay strong for them and try my hardest to talk these monsters out of not killing my family. But how could I possibly do that?

"If we stay here you might be spotted by the neighbors. Don't you think that it would be better if we left now while it's still dark. I was taken from you once before do you really want to take that chance?" I tried to plead with them the only way I knew how without showing my concern for my family. They looked at me and then at each other as if they were really contemplating my suggestion. But as soon as they looked at me, I knew they had already made their decision because Frank pulled out a gun and Susan pulled out a silencer. As she handed him the silencer and he put it on the gun he looked at me. "Don't you worry your pretty little head off. Your mother and I have already thought of everything we will be gone before the sunrise." I looked at my father and he was wide awake now. I wanted to hug him, I wanted to hug all of them. All I could do was look at my father pleading for an answer. There was only one thing his eyes were telling me, and I couldn't believe what they where saying. His eyes were telling me to "RUN."

How could I run away knowing that it would be the last time I would see my whole family alive? Shawn was crying and trying to say something but with the tape I couldn't understand what he was trying say. Frank walked up to my father and Susan walked up to my mother. As they stood behind my parents my heart dropped. I knew that I had run out of time. They were about to kill my parents. I couldn't hold back the tears anymore. Susan looked over at me and said "Darling you must stand behind the boy. He will be your first. I know that it will be hard at first but trust me it will get easier." I couldn't move a muscle.

Susan walked over to me took my hand and guided me over to Shawn. He looked so small so fragile. I didn't know what to do. I couldn't save my parents at all but there was a chance I could save Shawn. I looked over and Frank had the gun pointed at my father's head and I knew that he was going to pull the trigger any second. I looked my father in the eyes and mouthed 'I love you Daddy and I'm sorry.' With his eyes he told me he loved me too and then the gun went off. My father's head dropped. All I could hear was the muffled screams coming from my mother and Shawn.

I was in shock. It felt like I would collapse any second from now. My father the one that raised me and taught me everything I knew was now dead tied to a chair at the table my family and I have had so many meals and played so many board games. Who was I fouling? There was no way I could save anyone. Even though I have never met these two crazy insane people I felt as if all of this was my fault. Had my parents never adopted me they would not be in this situation. And now my father was dead, and I felt helpless and scared. I was not afraid for myself I was afraid for my mother and little brother. Frank handed the gun to Susan and she acted like a little schoolgirl. She was giddy and had a smile on her face that would have scared the devil himself. She put the gun up to my mother's head and looked at Shawn. Susan told him to say goodbye to his mommy and pulled the trigger. Our mothers head fell just as our fathers did and in the blink of an eye, we were orphans.

Shawn was crying hysterically trying to break from the tape. I did not know what I was going to do to protect him. I wanted to tell him that everything was going to be okay but I didn't want the last thing I said to my little brother to be a lie. I looked down at him seeing the tears fall from his cheeks and the fear in his eyes. It broke my heart to see him like this. These monsters were really doing this to an eight-year-old little boy. Was this the first child they ever did this to? It was unbearable seeing him like this and yet I was in so much shock that I could not even bring myself to cry. I knew that Shawn was next and that I had to do something to save him. But what would I be able to do? That's when Susan came up to me and handed me the gun and walked back over to Frank. There I was holding the gun that just killed my parents next to my little brother. That's when I found out what they wanted me to do. They wanted me to be the one to kill Shawn.

"Go on sweetheart its never easy the first time but it will be after this one." She said to me. I never looked up at them as she spoke to me, I was dumbfounded. "You want me to kill Shawn?" I asked without looking at them. "Well of course we do. We want to show you the way. You come from both of us and we know that you have it in you to do what is right." Frank said. He was right I did have the ability to do what was right, but it wasn't what he thought. Without hesitation I lifted the gun and pointed it at them. Within a second the gun went off shooting Frank in the stomach. I fired again and hit Susan in her chest.

They both fell to the floor and without hesitation I started to get Shawn out of the chair. As soon as I got him out, I told him to run to the neighbor's house and call the cops. "But what about you? You have to come with me Lilly I can't just leave you here alone with them. And I'm scared." I hugged him as tight as I could and bent down so that I could look at him eye to eye. "Shawn you have to do this by your self I'll be okay I swear to you. But the cops have to be called and I can't leave these monsters alone." He wrapped his arms around me and wouldn't let me go no matter how many times I tried to move his arms from around my neck. "Okay you don't have to go to the neighbor's just go up stairs into my room and get my cell phone. Can you do that for me please?" He finally let go and ran up to my room without saying a word.

I walked over to Frank and Susan. Frank was holding his stomach trying to stop the bleeding on his own. Susan was laying next to him unconscious or dead I couldn't really tell. I wanted her to be dead and I wanted him dead before the EMT's got there. But from the looks of it I was not going to be that lucky. He was looking at me like I betrayed him. But then he started to smile at me. And with a very faint voice he said "I knew you could kill just like your mother and me." And then he closed his eyes. I could tell he wasn't dead cause I could still see him breathing. I heard Shawn running back down the stairs and I stepped back in the spot that I was in when he had left. When he got to me, he handed me my cell phone with a shaking hand. I called 911 and told them exactly what happened, and they told me that they were on their way.

I looked at Shawn who was just standing there staring at our dead parent's and I knew that I had to get him out of the dinning room. So, I put my arm around his shoulders and brought him into the living room. He still had tears running down his cheeks and he was still shaking. I didn't know what I could do for him, so I put his favorite movie on and put a blanket around him. "Now stay right here and I'll go and get you some water." He didn't say a word he just grabbed me by the wrist and pulled me towards him. I sat down with him and held him until the cops showed up and knocked on the door. Shawn and I told them everything that had happened as Susan and Frank were brought out of the house. Susan was brought to the nearest hospital for surgery and Frank was brought out in a body bag. The one that had seemed so happy that I could shoot them was the one that would never say another word and I was grateful for that.

We were brought to the police department so that they could find out what they were going to do with us. They had us in a room and kept us in there. Periodically a police officer would come in and ask us if we needed anything or ask us more questions. A lot of the questions that they asked where the same questions just reworded I guess to see if we were lying about the events that took place. After a few hours of this my cell phone went off. I looked down at the caller id and saw that JoJo was calling me. I didn't know if I should answer it or not but to be honest I really needed my best friend right now.

"Hello." I said when I answered my phone. "Oh my god, Oh my god! Are you ok? Your house is all over the news. They're saying that they found three bodies in your house and another was brought to the hospital for surgery, but there not saying any names. What the hell is going on? Where are you right now?" Typical JoJo one hundred and one questions at one time without the possibility of answering her until she gets every one of them out. I could here the fear in her voice almost like she was about to cry. I took a deep breath and started to explain to her about everything that took place.

When I got to the part where my parents were gone she started crying. Both of our families were close. We went on almost every family vacation together. I told her that we were at the police station until they knew what to do with us. We stayed on the phone in silence for what seemed like forever. Finally she was able to bring herself to talk again. "What do you think there going to do with you two?" I told her the only thing I could think of what they would do.

"My only guess is that they will call social services and put us in foster care until we're eighteen. I mean what else can they do with us? We have no other family Mom and Dad were all that we had." Again the phone was silent as we both processed the fact that we might never see each other again. I started to cry again. These people these monsters have taken everything from me my parents and my whole life. At least I still had Shawn, the perfect combination of our parents. I swore to myself when he was born that I would always protect him and always take care of him.

I needed to keep that promise now more then ever. "Okay um I'm gonna get my parents caught up with everything that's going on and I'll give you a call back." She said finally. "Alright JoJo I'll let you know what's going on when I find out. And you'll call me whenever you find anything out right?" "I will I swear it." And with that we both hung up the phone. Shawn and I just sat in the little room waiting to see what the rest of our childhood would be.

We waited for what seemed like an eternity. Then one of the officers came in and said that there were some people that wanted to see us. We looked at each other in confusion and agreed to let them in. Our heads were down afraid that it was social services but when they walked in I jumped up and so did Shawn.

It was JoJo and her parents. We both ran to the three of them with tears in our eyes. I couldn't believe that they were right here with us but I was so grateful that they were. "What are you guys doing here?" I asked them. Mrs. Basher gently touched my shoulder and told the both of us to have a seat. We sat on the opposite side of the table and Mr. Basher got right into why they were here.

"First off let me say we cant express how sorry we are for your loss. Your parents where our best friends and we are all going to have to come to terms with what has happened. But, we all talked about it and we all agreed that we should all do that together." My head had been down this whole time up until he said 'together'. I looked up at them with tears in my eyes. Out of nowhere I felt someone's hand on mine and I looked over at JoJo and saw that it was hers. She was smiling and crying at the same time. I looked back over to her father and he continued what he was saying. "What I mean when I say together is we have an idea and we believe your parents would agree with us. We want you to come live with us and finish out your child hood with us." They all looked at us in anticipation on what our answer would be. JoJo chimed in just as I knew that she would and said "We can share a room and be like sisters. The thought of finishing high school without you seems horrible. You're my best friend and I look at Shawn as if he was my little brother as well. You just have to say yes."

Mrs. Basher put her hand on JoJo's and quietly said "Jody calm down now let them think about this for a minute. They have been through a lot and have a lot more to think about." She took a short pause and then looked at me. "Please know our hearts go out to you and we love you both to pieces. You always have and always will have a home with us. The decision is completely up to you but we wanted to know that we would love to have you. If you would like we can step outside and leave you both to think about what you two want." Before I could say anything to them Shawn grabbed me by the arm and said in a very soft voice "Can we stay with them please Lilith. I don't want to end up staying with people that we don't know. Not to mention I've heard a lot of really bad things about foster care. Please can we please?" That was the most he had spoke and how could I say no to people I thought of as my second family. "Of course we will. How could we say no?"

JoJo jumped up and hugged me as she screamed in my ear. What her opinion of an excited scream to the officers must have been bloody murder because one of the officers standing out side came storming in with a big look of worry on his face. We both kind of giggled that him and her mom apologized for having such a loud daughter. Mr. Basher went out to let them know we wanted to stay with them. A few hours later we were on our way to their house to get some rest. We were told that we would be able to go back to our house and collect our belongings the following day. Just the thought of going back there filled my heart with dread. So much so when we got to their house and they tucked us in I couldn't get even a minute of sleep. What had happened just kept running through my mind like the worst horror movie ever made. A couple of hours after we had all laid down I heard someone walking into the room. My heart dropped thinking of the worst. "Hello?" I whispered. The person walked up to the bed and then I knew it was Shawn. "Can I lay down with you please? I can't sleep." I moved over and lifted the covers. Shawn crawled into bed with me and we both just laid there wide awake until everyone else woke up.

The next day we went to our house and picked up our belongings. I went to my parents' room and grabbed my mothers and fathers wedding rings. They always put them on their nightstands when they went to bed. I also got two chains of my mothers. I put moms ring on one chain and dads on the other. I went to Shawn's room and put dads ring around his neck. I had moms around mine. When Shawn looked down to see what I put on him he put it in his hand and looked at me with a tear in his eye. We made a packed that we would wear them for the rest of our lives so that we would always have them with us.

As the years passed, I graduated from high school and went to collage for criminal justice. Shawn graduated from high school and went to collage for engineering. I joined the police department and was made the youngest homicide detective. I wanted to be the opposite from the monsters that took my parents from me. I wanted to bring justice to the victims of such horrible crimes. And now I have my shot to do so, and I vowed to not let anyone down no matter what I had to do.

Chapter 4

I had just got into bed when I got a call from my department informing me that I had a case. "We know that you requested the next two days off. But we really need you to come in now. I've already texted you the address." Rebeca said on the other side of the phone. I rolled my eyes, but I had to comply. Even after 10 years on homicide when they called, I had to come in. "Yeah, give me a few to get dressed and I'll be there in a bit. Has anyone touched anything yet?" I had to ask that because we had a new guy Todd that touched a murder weapon at the crime scene without gloves and almost destroyed the prints that where on it. I can't stand incompetence at all. "No ma'am no one has touched a thing just yet. They know to wait for you to get there. Oh, and Lilith just a heads-up Todd's there too. I'm sorry." She must have heard the sigh I slipped out when she said his name. She knew I didn't like him very much. And it wasn't really him it was the fact he was just a really bad detective and not all that smart. "It's fine Beca I'll be over there in a few." I said to her and hung up the phone.

On their ride over to the crime scene I started to wonder what kind of murder took place that I had to get my ass out of bed. I had just finished a case that involved a man killing little girls. I hope that psychopath get the death penalty. It was the worst crime scenes that I have ever seen. He chopped them up in different locations and bringing pieces of their bodies back to his house and cook them. He said it was to give him everlasting life and that he ate their hearts so that he could consume their souls. Every time I drive to a crime scene, I just keep asking in my head please please don't let it be a child. But what it was I would have never been able to comprehend. Hell, I still can't to this day.

I got out of my car and Todd came up to me and told me that the victim was a white male in his mid-thirties. "Did you touch anything at all Todd?" He gave me that look that a teenager gives their parents after they've been asked if they did something that they knew they weren't supposed to. "No detective I didn't touch anything." We started to walk into a church where the body was. I was looking around trying to see every little detail trying to see if anything was out of place. As we got closer to the body I froze in my tracks. I had to look up because the victim was hung on a cross. But I knew immediately knew who the person was just by the shoes he was wearing. The body on the cross was my little brother Shawn.

"When we get the body down well be able to see if he has any identification on him. Make it easier to identify the body and all that jazz." Todd said to me. I couldn't look away from Shawn. Whoever did this to him I was going to find. Only hard decision for me was to figure out if I was going to bring him into the station or kill the bastered myself. "We don't need ID to identify him." I said in a shacky voice. "You know him I take it?" Todd asked me. I nodded my head and said "Yeah I know him better then anyone in this world knows him. That's my little brother Shawn." Todd didn't know what to say which I was glad about cause if he tried to say anything I would more than likely have told him to shut up. I looked over everything that I needed to more so then ever before.

Further examination of the crime scene there was a note written on the floor in what I could only guess was my brothers' blood. Do not lie with a man as one lies with woman; that is detestable. So as of right now the only clue we had was that my little sweet brother was killed because he was gay. I still remember the day he came out to me. He was so afraid that I wasn't going to love him like I always had. He couldn't have been more wrong about that. In fact I loved him even more because I felt as if I was really seeing him for who he was. It made us even closer then ever before. Now he was gone, and I would never be able to have one of our long talks or one of our game nights again. I wanted this person who did this to him found so much more now with their little note.

"I want everything fingerprinted, bagged, whatever you can find I want it found." I went to go leave the church so that I could start making the proper phone calls. Todd stopped me when I was right at my car door "Do you need anything? Can I help you with anything?" I know that he was just trying to help but I was still trying to process what was going on and sometimes I can be a real bitch. "What you can do is DO NOT TOUCH ANYTHING!" He looked down at his hands and I realized that I needed to calm down a little bit. Todd was just trying to be a friend to me and I was being the worst person in the world. "I'm sorry Todd this is just really hard right now. I didn't need to snap at you, and I really didn't mean to." He looked up at me and smiled a little bit "I understand boss and if you need anything please don't hesitate to call."

The only thing I needed at this time was to know who killed my sweet little brother. On the drive to Shawn's house, I started to think back of when we were younger. Us playing video games, board games with the family, all the times he would creep into my room when he was scared. Then the memory of my sixteenth birthday when our parents died came flooding in my mind. The look in his eyes when he thought I was going to kill him. I told him later that the thought never crossed my mind. One way or another he was going to end up safe. And now he was gone. I had to pull over and regain my composure in order to finish my drive. The tears in my eyes where blinding me and making it impossible to see the road. "I just have to get to Shawn's house." I thought to myself. I wiped my tears away, took a deep breath, and continued to drive the last five miles I had to go.

When I got to Shawn's I just stood at the door for what seemed like forever. Every time I went to knock on the door I started to shake, and I would just stand there looking at the door. I took another deep breath and went to finally knock on the door when I heard it start to open. Shawn's boyfriend Jack was standing on the other side looking startled to see me standing there. "Lilith what are you doing here?" He asked me but before I could say anything to him, he started to talk again. "Shawn's not here. He hasn't been home all night I was actually on my way out to go look for him." As I went to tell him the news, he interrupted me again. "I know he was working late but he should have been home by now. I know he's probably just working a little later than normal."

Any time I tried to say something Jack would just start talking. I finally had to put my hand on his shoulder and say "Jack can I come in we need to talk." I could see the fear in his eyes and I think he could she the pain in mine. But, I had to tell him what was going on. I had to tell him that Shawn would not be coming home ever again. Jack moved to the side and motioned me to come inside. We sat down on the couch in silence for a little bit as I tried to come up with the words to tell him. "Jack something has happened to Shawn and I really don't know how to tell you but I think I should be the one you hear it from." Jack sat there and looked at me with tears in his eyes.

"Lilly, I know why you're here just tell me how it happened." I was in shock how would he know why I was there. "Ho....How do you know?" I finally broke down to ask him. "You're a detective in homicide and when I told you Shawn wasn't here you didn't look at all surprised. Then you asked me if we could come in and sit down. Not to mention you said something happened and I can see it in your eyes." He had a point I had to give him that. "You should be a detective, Jack." I joked. I always did that when I was uncomfortable. "Shawn's been murdered and hung up in a church. The only clue that we have is he was killed for being gay." When I said it out loud to Jack, I broke down crying. Jack hugged me and we stayed in that embrace for a while. Not knowing what else we could say to each other.

Jack finally got up from the couch and asked me if I wanted a drink. "You got everclear and grape soda?" I asked him. "This is Shawn's house of course we have that." We both chuckled a little bit, I think we where both thinking about all the times Shawn would get drunk during any party they would throw and start dancing like a fool. He was always so funny because he was the worst dancer anyone had ever seen. But everyone loved him. I even think people came to the parties just to see him dance. Looking back at that I started to feel the tears coming back and Jack went to go and get our drinks.

We sat there in the living room for the whole night talking about Shawn and what an amazing man he was. We laughed, we cried, we even sat there in silence thinking about him. By the end of the night, I was too drunk to drive home and Jack offered to let me stay on the couch. I knew there was no way I would be able to drive so I accepted his offer. I dreamt of the night our parents were killed. A nightmare I haven't had in years but this time it was worse. After our parents where killed the scene changed to the church and Shawn was hanging there where I had found him. My parents where standing next to me with there hands on my shoulders. "Why couldn't you protect him?" our mother asked me. "That's the only thing that we asked of you with our last thoughts." our father said. Then Shawn looked down at me and spoke. "I was your little brother and you always promised me that nothing would ever happen to me." I woke up screaming his name and apologizing.

Jack was right by my side he was about to try and wake me up. "Lilly it's ok I'm here. It was just a bad dream." For a second, I thought it was Shawn and I hugged him and started to tell him about my nightmare. When I called Jack Shawn, he quickly reminded me of the events from the night before. I had such a hang over it took me a minute for everything to make since to me again. Shawn was gone and I was in his home with the love of his life. "Its ok Lilly its ok." With the sound of Jacks words, I just started to cry. Nothing was fine and nothing was ever going to be fine again. My whole family was gone and now it was my responsibility to find out who had done this to my little brother. I would never again have my best friend by me when I had a tough case, or I broke up with a boyfriend.

I looked at Jack after I was done crying and just said "I know." I sat up on the couch and looked at my cell phone. I thought I would at least have one call about my brothers' case but there was nothing there. Jack had gotten up and went to go make us some coffee. Something I think that we both needed at this time. I saw the bottle on the table "Man we drank almost the whole thing last night" I said to myself. No wonder why I was so hungover. I knew the medicine for a hangover was a bite from the snake that bite you, so I grabbed the bottle and took a shot. As soon as it touched my tongue I felt sick to my stomach but got it down. As soon as I did Jack came in with the coffee and looked sick. "You ok their Jack you look sick." He took a moment before he answered me and then finally said "I also have a hangover and the thought of how that stuff taste is gross." I chuckled at him a little cause I knew how he felt. "Yeah, I know trust me but if I'm gonna get started on this case I really need this hangover to go anywhere else but here."

He looked at me with concern something I had already anticipated. Shawn and him both knew that I was a workaholic. But this was a different story this was my little brother. Jack handed me my cup of coffee and sat down. I knew that he was going to try to talk me out of going in, but nothing was going to stop me from doing that. "Lil, I got a call from your boss. And I know that you're going to hate what I'm about to tell you, but this is their protocol." I knew what he was going to say and even though I didn't want to hear it I knew he was going to tell me anyways. "You're off Shawn's case. You're to close to..." He was trying to get the word victim out, but he just started to tear up. "Jack, you don't have to finish your sentence I know what you're trying to tell me."

I was trying to stay calm about the situation, but I was just getting more and more pissed off. I knew that as soon as my boss found out that Shawn was my brother, he would take me off the case. But how could I just stand by and not find his killer. Humans have an extremely hard time to process the untimely death of a loved one and it can make it more difficult for us to think clear minded. Especially when we're trying to solve a murder of said loved one. I knew that I had to at least go talk to my boss about this. At least get information as the police department did. "He doesn't want you to come in for a few days. He also wants you to go see the departments psychiatrist." It seemed that he said the last part with hesitation. "I know that's what's supposed to happen when we have to deal with something like this. I'm gonna go into the office and have a talk with him. And I'll be damned if I'm going to see the shrink. I did that when I our parents died, I don't want to do that again."

I knew that Jack was just trying to help me, but I didn't want to listen. There was no way in hell I was going to be left in the dark and see a shrink. Jack looked at me while he shook his head and said, "Well go see him if you must but remember this if you need someone to talk to or need a place to crash my door is always opened." He was such a caring person and only wanted the best for anyone. I understood what he lost I had lost the same thing. A sweet loving man with a heart of gold. "Look if it makes you feel any better, I will go to the shrink but I also going to go see my boss to make sure I get all the information found on the case." I thought that would make him feel better but the look in his eyes were filled with worry. But instead of him speaking his concern he just took my hand into his and said, "You do whatever you think is best but please go see the psychiatrist."

When he put my hand into his it gave me flash backs of when my father would do the same. I wanted to cry again but I held back my tears and stood up. As I started to walk to the door Jack got up to see me out. We gave each other a hug and stood there for a moment. "You know Shawn loved you more then anything. I think he even loved you more then he loved me." I said to him. He started to cry and said "No Lilly his love for you was way greater. I know he didn't get a chance to tell you this, but he had just asked me to marry him a couple of days ago. We were going to tell you this weekend." He showed me the ring that Shawn had given him. I looked at the ring and then at him. I placed my hand on his shoulder and gave him a kiss on his forehead just like I would do to Shawn. I walked out of the door without another word. I had no idea what I should say. The news was shocking and hurtful because they would never get their special day. They had the type of love that you could see last forever, and it was taken away by some lowlife asshole. An asshole I would find one way or another.

I decided that I was going to go home and shower before I went to go see my boss. The ride home unfortunately made me pass by the church where Shawn was killed. I almost crashed into a car that was stopped at a red light when I passed by it. I just couldn't take my eyes off of it. As my car came to a screeching halt, I felt the overpowering sensation to cry. The person in the car in front of me flipped me off but I couldn't care less. For the rest of the ride, I felt as if I was in a trance. I didn't even remember driving from that red light to my apartment. Somehow, I was able to park my car and walk up to my door. I finally came to my senses when I put the key in the door. I brushed it off and walked inside. I went to the kitchen to go get something to drink. I got a soda out of the fridge and then without thinking about it I went to the cupboard where I kept my liquor. I brought the liquor, a shot glass, and the soda into the living room and sat down in front of the tv.

I sat there for a moment or two trying to figure out what to do next. I mean it was obvious that I was going to sit down and drink but why. I knew what I had to do and here I was with a bottle on the table right in front of me and the only thing I could think about doing was drinking it. I grabbed the tv remote and looked for something to watch. I thought to myself if I just focused on a movie or a tv show then maybe I wouldn't drink. But as I was flipping through the channels, I came across the last movie that me and my family watched together. I sat there starring at the tv having flash back of all those that where no gone. How could I deal with all of this? How was one person supposed to live life with everything thing that I have been through in my life and still feel normal? Without even thinking I grabbed the bottle and poured me a shot. Before I knew it half of the bottle was gone, and the movie was halfway over. It seemed as if I wasn't in control of my actions. I kept pouring shot after shot. The next thing I remembered was waking up on my couch with yet another hangover and another almost empty bottle.

I slowly got up because every movement I did made my head pound. I went to pour me a shot to help take away the hangover and saw blood on my sleeve. I sat there for a while staring at them looking over my arms and my hands but there was no more blood anywhere else. I finished pouring the shot and forced it down. Then I went into the bathroom to see if the blood could have come from my noise. I used to get really bad bloody noises when I was younger, and I could have come from that. But when I looked in the mirror, I saw nothing on my face. Could I have came into the bathroom while I was drunk and cleaned my face off? That seemed like the only logical explanation. I turned the shower on and started to get undressed. I think that was the longest shower I have ever taken in my life. As I was just about to get out and dry off my cell phone rang. I grabbed my towel and ran straight to my phone.

I answered it and it was Rebecca. "Curtis was wanting to know when you were going to come in and see him." 'The boss man just couldn't give me a couple of days could he.' I thought to myself. "I'm so sorry for your loss." She said when I didn't reply to her. "Thank you and yes I'm coming in. I just got out of the shower. Let him know I will be there in about thirty minutes." I finally said to her. "Hey, I know that I'm not to really say anything to you right now about any new cases, but we had another victim almost the same as your brother. I don't know any more details than that, but I thought that I would let you know." Serial Killers weren't very well known in our area but there's a first time for everything. "I'm on my way now just gotta get dressed." Without even waiting for a goodbye, I went ahead and hung up the phone. After I got dressed, I ran to the fridge to find a quick bite only to find it was empty. 'I really need to go get groceries' I thought to myself. And went right out the door.

As soon as I pulled into the station, I regretted my decision of showing up in the first place. I knew that the whole department knew about Shawn and I really didn't want anyone mentioning it. Unless someone had information on his case and was willing to share it with me that is. Anytime someone dies in your family everyone wants to say, "I'm sorry for your loss." I never understood that, and I always hated it. Now I had the whole police department aware of my loss. And that one woman that's worked here for twenty years and for the life of me I can never remember her name. But she always makes a casserole or something like that whenever someone in the department losses someone. Like who the hell wants to eat casserole after someone close to them dies. I can't even avoid everyone.

How would I? Leave the department with no notice and try to start somewhere new? And with that thought I sat in my car looking at the department thinking about doing just that. I burst out laughing with the thought. Realizing that was the first time I have laughed since the last time I saw Shawn and Jack. I never really laughed since our parents died. I was always the serious one and Shawn was the joker. But he always knew how to make me laugh and I was always grateful for that. And now my joker was gone, and I felt guilty for laughing without him. I took a deep breath, got out of the car, and took that long walk into the department. As I walked in everyone turned to look at me and I saw the look in their eyes. The look of sympathy that I saw made me want to leave so bad. If it weren't for the fact I had to talk to Curtis or the fact I wanted to see if there was any update on Shawn's case I would have just walked right out.

I did the only thing that I could do. I continued to walk with my head held high. Trying not to look at anyone as I passed through the department. I could feel their eyes on me even when I couldn't see them. I could hear the sound of whispers moving through the department. I knew that they were talking about me and I was never one for anyone to talk about me. I did the only logical thing I could think of. I stood on top of the desk and shouted loud enough for everyone in the department to hear me. "Alright everyone listen up. I want to say in advance thank you to everyone that wants to give their condolences on my brother's death. No, I do not need anything from anyone except for my privacy. And please stop with the whispers about it. I'm perfectly fine and capable of dealing with this on my own. Thank you for your time." With that I stepped of and walked straight to the boss's office where his was sitting at his desk shaking his head. Right there I knew that I may or may not have crossed a small line.

Chapter 5

"Okay okay I know how that looked." I said as I put my hands up like someone being held at gun point. Before I could say anything, else Curtis motioned for me to sit down. I did as I was instructed to do. I really didn't want to be here and listen to what ever it was that he had to say. I've been through a big loss before, and I had to witness it. Only difference was with this loss is that I didn't see it take place. "Look I'm really not worried about that right now. The only thing I am worried about is you getting checked with the shrink so I can get you back out there." That took me for a loop when he said that to me. We never wanted anyone to try and rush right back into work. I mean normally someone in my case would be requested to take two weeks off with pay.

"You know I could just skip the shrink crap and come straight back to work right?" I said sarcastically but with a little bit of hope that he would actually allow me to do that. "Don't be a smartass White you know I can't allow that. And even if I could after that little display, I wouldn't even think about it." He looked at me as if he were trying to look right through me. Which is what he always did when he was frustrated. He rubbed his eyes as he sat up in his chair and put his hands together on his desk. "You know that you have to at least be evaluated and depending on what they say depends on how fast you can come back."

I didn't even care about having to go and get an evaluation done all I cared about was finding out about Shawn's case. And what the similarities where with the other body that they found. As soon as I opened my mouth to try and ask Curtis interrupted me. "There are no new developments on your brother's case as of right now. And as soon as we find any, we will let you know as much as we are able to tell you. But as you know we can't give you any suspects names when we do find them." Even though that infuriated me I knew that he was only telling me the truth. I was to close to the victim so I was only allowed to know what a normal family member could know. I also knew that the only thing I could do was to be cleared from the shrink and start on the new case that Curtis wanted me to start on.

I called and made the appointment for the following day. So that made it to where the rest of the day was mine and there was only one thing I had to take care of. I had to start planning Shawn's funeral. I called Jack as soon as I got into my car. As soon as he answered I felt nothing but regret for even thinking about having the conversation we were about to have. "Hey, um I was just wondering if you wanted to help with the planning for Shawn?" I asked him as soon as he said hello. He took a moment to answer not that I could blame him. "Sure, Lil I would be honored to." I didn't want to stay on the phone with him only because I felt so bad. This wasn't the event he was supposed to be planning. Him and Shawn should be sitting in their house right now planning their wedding. And now this poor sweet man has to burry his love. "Okay I'll be over in about an hour, and we can start everything. Bye." I said and hung up the phone before he had a chance to speak.

Where did I go when I got of the phone with Jack you might ask? Well, I went to the damn liquor store. There was no way I would be able to deal with this sobber. And honestly, I don't think Jack would be able to either. I got two bottles of rum one for myself and one for me and Jack. I've never really been a heavy drinker but, this shit was just getting to me to bad. There wasn't a moment of my day I didn't think about it. And every time I would think about it, I wanted to have a drink. I didn't want to feel this pain at all. Drinking was the only way I wouldn't feel it while I was awake. But as soon as I fell asleep the dreams would start and I would feel even worse. Almost every time I would see my parents. It was horrifying because I could see the holes in their heads from where the monster's shot them. My mother would be holding Shawn's body and cry. I could see her tears fall on his pale face as she screamed at me. "How could you let this happen?" And my father next to her screaming "You were supposed to protect him!" And the monster behind them laughing and motioning for me to go with them.

Yeah, I was definitely going to need a good amount of therapy. The real question would be 'would I actually go?' Probably not. I've always been very stubborn and not in a good way. I think that's why I can never have a relationship. It was either that or my job. Getting called in all hours of the night. And don't get me started when I'm on a case I bring my work home and don't rest a whole lot until I solve the crime. I only had one unsolved case that is now in our cold case files. But every two years I look at it again and see if I missed anything. So far from what I've seen I haven't. This year is the year I would go back and look at it again. But that won't happen until Shawn's case is solved. I felt bad for the family. You see it was a little kid that got kidnapped straight out of her bed. When we found her body you could barley recognize her. I never caught the ass hole that did it but mark my words one day I will. And he's going to regret his entire life decisions.

When I got to Jack's and Shawn's I just sat there just like when I pulled into the department. I started to think about the fact that Shawn wasn't going to be there. I grabbed the bottle that I had bought for myself, and I took a nice big swig of it. I almost didn't get it down before I got my chaser, but I pushed through it. I looked up at the house and saw Jack standing on the stoop outside his house just staring at my car. I figured that he was contemplating on whether or not to come and check on me. And that's when I saw him walking down the steps. I quickly hid my bottle and grabbed the bag with our bottle in it and stepped out of the car. Jack was giving me a worried look but didn't ask me any questions. "I know creepy sitting in my car in front of your house ain't it." I said and he smirked. We met half way between his house and my car and he turned around as he put his arm around my neck.

"I got us a bottle for tonight." I said to him as I lifted it up in the air. "Well, you know what they say? Great minds think a like because I went to the store earlier and got us a bottle since the last one mysteriously disappeared." We looked at each other and laughed. When we got inside, I could see that Jack ordered dinner for us and I could see the bottle that he was talking about. We both sat down and started to put food on a plate. It was my favorite Japanese food Sushi from my favorite place. I put my plate on the table and Jack followed suit. We just sat there in silence for a little while before he grabbed the bottle and poured us both a shot. We took the shot, and I knew it was my turn to pour but before I was able to get it Jack had grabbed it and started to pour the next one.

I could tell that we wouldn't really get anything done tonight even though we had to. But who could blame us? I guess a lot of people could because a lot of people go through this type of thing but we weren't like normal people. We got about half way through the bottle and got about half of what we needed to get done for Shawn's funeral. Jack looked up at me and told me that we were done with the planning for the night. I agreed of course, I mean I really didn't want to continue doing this shit. One thing that some people my not understand is that planning an event like this is just a reminder that your loved one is gone. And that is something that neither one of us wanted to remember. I mean the reminder was all around us as it was. Shawn should be here making dumb ass jokes and dancing around, but he wasn't and the silence let us know that.

Jack got up to put on music to try and to make the mood better but it really didn't work. Shawn was the one that always wanted to listen to music and hearing it only made us miss him even more. I knew that I was to drunk to drive home so I went to call a cab. But Jack wasn't having it at all. "You're gonna stay here tonight. Because if you go home then you'll have to call another cab to come and get your car. And that makes no since to do that when you can stay right here." He did have a point even though I really didn't want to stay there. And it wasn't because of Jack it was because when I woke up I knew that my brother wouldn't be the one to bring me a cup of coffee. But to make him happy I decided to stay the night.

The next morning I woke up with yet another hangover. It made me think 'Why do people drink excessively?' When I stood up I could hardly hold myself up correctly. I went to use the bathroom and start the coffee knowing that Jack drank more then me, I knew he would be getting up a little later then me. Just as I turned the coffee pot on Jack came in the kitchen. He looked like he just walked through hell three times over. He sat down at the bar and put his head on the table. "Damn man you look like you did a little partying all night or you got ran over by a train." I teased him. He lifted his head just enough to give me a dirty look and put his head back down. I went into the living room and poured us a shot to get rid of our handover. When I put it in front of him he groaned and pushed it away. "Nope we both have to take one. We have a hangover and you know just as well as I do that this is the best way to get rid of it." We both looked at the shot glasses like an enemy but got both of them down with little to no problems. As soon as the coffee was done I proud both of us a cup and we sat in the kitchen and just drank our coffee in silence. Shortly after that I had left to go to my apartment and get ready for the day.

When I got to my apartment first thing I did was grab the bottle that I had got the night before and a chaser. Second thing I did was go straight to my couch and pour a shot. I knew that I didn't have to see the shrink for another two days so I couldn't work. So I decided to sit at home watch tv and drink until I passed out. I knew that it wasn't the best thing in the world to do but, it was the only thing that I wanted to do. The time seemed to pass by because when I got up to use the bathroom I noticed that the sun had gone down. The last thing I remember was walking back to the living room and sitting down, after that I must of past out drunk. The next morning I woke up and went to the bathroom and I couldn't believe what I was seeing in the mirror. I got as close as I could to the it staring at myself. It was like something out of a horror movie. I had blood all over me. You could have mistaken me for Carrie from that movie. I looked over my body yet again to try and find out if there was any gashes on my body and I couldn't find one. I had so many questions going through my head and couldn't find the answers to them. "WHAT THE HELL IS GOING ON?"

I got in the shower and cleaned up. I couldn't understand for the life of me what was going on. The last thing I remembered was sitting down on my couch. What in the world happened? I was so freaked out I was shaking. Just as I got out of the shower I could hear my phone ringing but I didn't care at all who it was. I got dressed and went back into the living room. The phone rang again yet I didn't look at it. I picked it up and put it on silence without ever looking at the screen. I wanted to find out what was going on but how could I do that if I couldn't remember anything from last night. I sat there on the couch staring at the bottle that wasn't even have gone for what seemed like hours until I heard a knock at the door. I chose not to answer it simply because I didn't want to see anyone. After the third knock I thought that who ever it was would leave. But then I heard a key going into the lock and I automatically grabbed my gun and pointed it at the door and pulled the trigger.

"Whoa whoa Lil it's just me don't shoot." I stood there shaking because I almost shot Jack. I forgot that I gave Shawn a key a while back when I first moved in. I almost shot the only person that could really connect me to Shawn. The only family I really had left. Jack came running up to me after I put the gun down and wrapped his arms around me. I broke down and started crying. "Lil what's going on the department has been trying to call you and so have I. I came right over when they called me and said that you never showed up to your appointment." He slowly helped me sit on the couch and I looked at him in shock. "I don't have that appointment for tomorrow. I never missed it." I could see the concern in his eye's and he said "Sweety your appointment was this morning."

How could have I missed a whole day. It didn't make any since at all. Now I'm having black out spells to where I'm missing days?. When was going to be the next time? And how do I explain all the blood all over my clothes and body? I didn't want to deal with this on my own and I knew that there was no way that I could. "I've got to show you something Jack and please don't freak out." I knew that when I sad that he was going to worry. I went into the bathroom without waiting on his response and gathered my bloody clothes and brought them to him. "I don't know what is going on but I woke up with these clothes on this morning. The last thing I remember was coming back to the couch two nights ago apparently. I don't know what is going on and I'm petrified to find out. But I don't know who in the world to go to other than you." I could see the fear in his eyes as he unfolded the bloody clothes.

"What happened? What is this Lil?" He asked me and all I could do was break down and cry some more. How could I explain something to him that I couldn't understand myself? I just sat there shaking my head. He put his hands on my face and forced me to look at him. "Lilith where did those clothes come from. Those are the same ones you were wearing when you left my house. Ain't they?" I took a deep breath and finally said "I don't know what happened like I said. I don't know what to do. No matter how hard I try I can't remember what happened in those 48 hours. I need help but I don't even know the type of help that I need." Jack finally let go of my face and pored us a shot. We both took it and sat there in silence for a while.

"Ok why don't you take the clothes to the crime lab and get them to identify who the blood belongs to? That should be able to give you a clue of what happened." I had already thought about that but the amount of blood that was on my clothes who ever the blood belonged to couldn't still be alive. I told Jack all of that and that I was afraid that I killed someone in my sleep. But if that was so how could that have happened. I have never slept walked before. Jack decided to throw an idea at me that I really needed a shot after I heard it. "What if we wash the clothes not in bleach just to get all your DNA off of it and then bring it in. I mean like put it in a garbage bag and tell them you found it. Would that work?" I thought about it for a minute and decided that his idea was my only option. We took another shot got some tape and got all the hair off of the clothes and then washed them. We made the plan that he was going to bring them into the precinct for me and just say that he found them. Hoping that the department wouldn't be able to tell if it was my clothes. It was the only real shot I had. As I sat there looking at Jack I was trying to figure out why he would help me like this. Then I thought about it and Jack was the only family that I had left just as I was the only family that he had left.

Jack's family refused to have anything to do with him after he came out to them over 10 years ago. When him and Shawn met that's one thing that they defiantly had in common. When Shawn came out to JoJo and her family they all did the same thing to him. If my brother wasn't good enough for them neither was I. So we all went our separate ways and never spoke again. That was 5 years ago this Christmas. We didn't need them any ways we had each other. But poor Jack had to go 5 years before he met Shawn all by himself. Yeah he had boyfriends in the past but him and Shawn where one of a kind. I feel so bad knowing he'll never find a love like that again.

I looked at Jack sitting on my couch and poured us a shot. We both lifted our glasses at the same time. "Here's to family." I said to him with a wink and a clink of the glasses we took our shot. We drank all night listening to music and playing stupid drinking games. We ended up finishing the bottle off and passing out on the couch. The next morning we woke up at the same time. Jack looked at the bottle and noticed it was empty. "Well looks like we're gonna have to deal with these hangovers all day." He said and if I didn't know any better I would have sworn that there was a hint of relief in his voice.

"Don't worry brother I got you. I mean who's house do you really think you're in right now." I got up which was not an easy task with my head pounding but, I pulled through it and went to my freezer. I got out the small bottle I had in there and looked at it. There was enough for two shots and I handed it over to Jack while I went to the bathroom. "You know I don't remember the last time that I drank this much." He said loud enough for me to hear him as he poured our shots. I came back out as he took his shot. "Went down a little hard didn't it?" I asked him. He just nodded his head and got up to go make coffee. I took my shot like I was craving it. I knew that today was going to be the day that

Jack brought my cloths to the office. And I knew that we would both be on edge till we found out what happened to them.

"So how do you want to go about doing this?" I asked him while we was bringing the coffee cups to the table. "Just as I said last night. I'll bring them into the office and say that I found them behind that trash at work." I looked at him confused. "I thought I was going to bring them in." He smirked behind his coffee cup. "I thought you were a detective Lil." I went to say something and he put his hand over mine. "Lil you don't ever bring your own evidence." "But I didn't do anything wrong Jack. I couldn't have." I said to him and I could feel the fear in my voice. "We don't know what happened but one way or the other you got a good amount of blood all over your clothes there's no telling what happened. I just want to be I'm not saying you did anything wrong I just want to be safe."

I understood where he was coming from but at the same time I wanted him to stay safe as well. Before I had a chance to say anything to him to try and protest he got up from the couch. "Well I'm gonna get to work I'll drop the clothes off when I get off. And then I'll go pick up some dinner for us and meet you back here." I looked at him dumbfounded. "What do you mean you'll meet me back here?" I asked him. "I'm not letting you stay by yourself until we find out what the hell is going on with you. And I'm not gonna hear anything about it either. Right now you're stuck with me wither you like it or not." He gave me a kiss on my forehead and headed for the door with the bag of bloody clothes.

"Love ya sis." He sad as he was walking out the door. That was the first time he had ever said that to me let alone kissing me on my forehead. I was in shock, so much so that when my alarm went off I jumped out of my seat. I had the appointment with the shrink in an a couple of hours so I decided to take a shower and get ready to go. I couldn't shake off how odd Jack had been but I knew I could trust him with my life. And in a way that's exactly what I was doing. Another alarm went off while I was in the shower which got me out of my daze. I jumped out of the shower and finished getting ready.

Chapter 6

I got to the office and already dreaded being there. The last time I saw a shrink my parents had just been killed by my birth parents. And now I'm here because my little brother was killed because he loved another man. I knew the first question this person was going to ask was 'How are you doing?' How am I supposed to answer that question without exploding at the shrink? How am I supposed to be feeling right now? I'm angered, I feel nothing but hate in my heart right now. The only bad feeling I didn't feel was alone I had Jack the last bit of feeling that I had. So I decided I needed to focus on that. I one good feeling I had left.

A woman come out of the room and called my name. I stood up and she said "Follow me." as she pointed the way in to her office. I just thought to myself 'Great a woman they are always caught up in their feelings. This isn't gonna be as easy as I thought.' I sat down on the loveseat that she had and just waited patently for the question I knew she was going to ask. "Ms. White how are you doing today. I know you just lost your brother and that you were at the scene of the crime. That must have been very hard for you to see." I looked at her and took a deep breath "Not any harder then seeing your parents murdered right in front of you." I said without even thinking.

"You saw your parents murdered in front of you when did this happen?" Great me and my big mouth had to open that can of worms that I didn't want to open. "It happened when I was 16 years old and I've already seen on of you about that when I was younger. So with all do respect I really don't want to talk about their murder just my brothers. And yes to answer your question that was very hard to see. My brother and I are the only ones left in our family. Well I guess I'm the only one left now." I said to her. I meant all the respect in the world when I said that to her. I really didn't want to talk about my parents. What happened to them is the reason I got into the profession that I am in now. And I really think they would be proud of me for it.

"Ok that's fine we're only here for what ever you want to talk about. Where are my manners today? Ms. White my name in Annabel Sanchez and you can call me Ann." She had one of those soft voices that you would imagine for a shrink. I noticed her long jet black hair in a tight bun and thought 'that must give her bad headaches by the end of the day.' Her green eyes reminded me of a vampire movie that Shawn made me watch when we were kids. Though I couldn't for the life of me remember the movie. And she had pale white skin just like a vampire would. 'Why am I thinking about vampires right now?' I thought to myself.

"Well Ann you can call me Lil everyone else does." I said with a smirk. "Ok Lil how do you feel about your brothers murder?" I looked at her with a now confused look. What kind of dumbass question was that to ask. How do I feel about it I freaking pissed that's how I feel. I cant go one night without drinking till I cant feel anymore cause if I don't I dream about it. Is this bitch for real right now? I take a deep breath so I don't say anything that would keep me from my job any longer and answered "I feel hurt from my community. I feel that in this day and age we shouldn't be killing people for loving who they love. That's how I feel."

She looked at me with pity in her eyes and god damn do I ever hate people pitying me. "Ok I can understand that and I completely agree with you." "Look doc let me make this easy for you do I miss my brother goddess yes I do. Am I sad that he's gone yes every time I think about it I feel sadder and sadder. Do I want revenge to the ass holes that did this to him no. The only thing I want is justice for my kid brother who was taken way to soon." She wrote some stuff down and looked back up at me. "Normally when we have cases like this the family member involved normally want revenge. It takes a very big person to want justice over revenge." "I'm a homicide detective I know what happens when you get revenge you get your freedom taken from you as well. And there is no one in this world that is worth taking away my freedom for."

I know that I had pain in my voice but what I also had was certainty. "Yes, my brother was gone but if I were to be taken away where would that leave the man that he loved? It would leave poor Jack alone without anyone that cares for him. And I'll be damned if he's going to come see me in jail or prison." She wrote down some more stuff. God I hate it when they did that shit. "So Jack is?" She asked. "Jack was my brothers' fiancé of one week. They where together for 5 years shortly after my brother came out to me. He's the only family that I really have left. And he's the one that has been there for me through all of this."

"So you and Jack are close?" she asked me as she was writing some more stuff down. "Just about as close as me and Shawn was." "It's good that you have someone that can help you through this time." She said. As she's going through her notes and I'm just sitting there going through the motions she finally lifts her head from her little notebook and say "I think were done here. I've got all I need for your reinstatement just give me a few minutes and we should be good to go." I looked at her in shock. Normally I would have to sit here for an hour getting in touch with my feelings and she's just letting me go back to work. This was just completely awesome. "Ok." I simply said and I sat there waiting for my paperwork.

She handed me the paperwork and wished me a good day and I said the same to her and walked out the door. I saw the all clear on my paperwork and couldn't be happier. I was headed out the door of the building as by boss was walking in. I handed her the paper and said "See Chief I'm all good to go can I come back to work now or are you going to make me go so crazy I end up needed to see Miss Sanchez all the time." She looked at the paper and said go down to the precinct and see what they got. But I beg of you stay away from Shawn's case." I didn't know what to say to her at the time. Of course I would check on the case it was Shawn for crying out loud.

"Of course not you're the captain captain." I said with a salute and left to get in my car to head to the office. I wanted nothing more right now then to sit behind my desk and breath in the smell of crime and bad coffee. I jumped in my car and as soon as I turned my car on my cell rang. I answered it without even seeing who it was. "Hi, jack how are you? Or should I say how is your hangover?" I could hear him moan in disgust. "Not funny Lil not funny at all. How was your appointment?" I didn't remember if I told Jack or not so it surprised me that he asked that. "I'm not crazy, well at least not that Dr. Sanchez can see." I joked "Of course they would look over you being crazy. Listen I wanted to let you know that I dropped those clothes off on my lunch break. Boy they give strange looks at you when you bring bloody clothes in that have been washed. Or is it just the fact that they where bloody I don't know."

"I think it would be the fact that they're bloody goof ball." I said to him and we both laughed. I don't think that either one of us knew why we were laughing the fact that I had blood all over my clothes and no idea where it came from really was no laughing matter. But when you can't cry you laugh right? We sat there on the phone in silence for a few minutes until I said "Well I'm about to go to the office now so I will see you when you get to the apartment." "Ok Lil I love you." This time I wasn't as shocked as I was this morning and I said the only thing I could think of "I love you too bye." I hung up the phone and headed to the station.

When I got to the office I wasn't worried about the looks or the whispering that happened before. I was just going to put it in the back of my mind and get back to work. To my surprise no one looked at me with the pity eyes or whispered about me to one another. It was peaceful and I really appreciated them all for the respect. I got to my desk and sat down and just basked in the aroma of the bad coffee with my eyes closed. It felt like I was home like I belonged here. You never really know how much you love your job until you cant be there for a while. And boy did I love my job.

Todd came up to my desk and handed me a file. I opened my eyes and looked at the front of the folder. "What's this Todd?" I asked him and he just stood there. "Todd what the hell is this did you forget to speak or something?" I was getting irritated. I mean when I ask you a question answer the damn question, please. "That's the two murders that happened while you were out. We believe that it's the same unsub." He finally answered. I looked through the file and there was something oddly familiar with the crime scene, but I couldn't but my finger on what it was.

"Is that all that you need Todd or is there something else I can help you with?" I asked with a little venom in my voice. I really didn't mean to but this guy always irked me. He was a horrible detective and common since was not a friend of his. "Captain wants me to work with you on this case. You know for some additional training?" He said. Great now I got this ass hole to babysit. Out of nowhere another officer was rushing over to my desk with paperwork in his hand. As he handed it to me I didn't even have enough time to ask him what it was about. "There where some clothes covered in blood that someone brought in today and they match with the second victim." I just sat there in shock when I saw the paperwork because along with the DNA test was a picture of the clothes. A picture of my clothes that Jack had brought in not to long ago.

How did my clothes match the DNA of the second victim of this case. Did I kill this person and have no recollection of it. That was impossible wasn't it? Well the only thing to do now was to go home after work and talk to Jack about it. Good thing for us I brought my work home with me. I went over all of the case file and couldn't place why I would be there. Todd was starting to get on my nerves asking me dumb questions like "Who do you think did it?" Why do you think they did it?" "How the hell am I supposed to know Todd I just started on the case today it doesn't work like that. You can't just look at a case file and automatically know who or why. If it was that easy, we would both be out of a job." I really didn't mean to snap on him but at least he was quite the rest of the day.

At 5 o'clock I decided to head home I knew that Jack would be there waiting on me with possibly cold food by know. I stopped at the liquor store on my way home and sure enough Jack was there when I got there. I walked into the apartment with the bag from the liquor store which contended two bottles of rum. And there he was sitting on my couch with the Chinese food on the coffee table and two shot glasses along with a bottle that had already been opened. "I see that you started without me." I said to him before placing the bottles in the freezer. "I guess I did." He said as he grabbed the bottle and poured us a shot. "Okay I'll take this one and then I gotta run down to the car I have information about the clothes that you're not going to believe." I took the shot and headed out the door.

I got back and sat down next to him pulling the file that I copied from the office out of my bag. "The clothes have a DNA match that's from the last victim of this case that I'm on." I said to him. He sat there staring at the picture of my clothes like he couldn't believe what I had just said. "Ok..... So we need to figure out why you were there and what you had done." He said as he poured us a shot and got our dinner out of the bag. I was wrong about the food being cold it was nice and warm.

Chapter 7

As we ate our food, we looked through the case file. I couldn't understand why they had both of these men in one case file. I couldn't find one thing that would connect them to one another. Then we got to the pictures, and I froze and started to shake. "What's wrong Lil?" It took me a few minutes to answer him. In fact I didn't answer him until he put his hand on my shoulder. "They were killed the same way that Shawn was." I said and he just looked at the pictures. When I could finally bring myself to stop starring at them I looked up at Jack. I knew that this affected him because now he was seeing how the love of his life was killed in such a brutal and hateful manner.

I took the pictures to see if there was something about their deaths other then being hung on a cross and that's when I saw the bible quote. 'Thou shall not kill.' One of the ten commandments. They both had it written in their own blood. I closed the file and placed it on the table. When I looked over to Jack he was crying. I put my arms around him, we sat there and cried for a while. We finally let each other go and took a shot in honor of Shawn and I put the file away. I noticed that the two victims had one thing other thing in common that Shawn did not. There message was both 'Thou shall not kill'. But if that was their message, who did they kill?

"What the hell is going on Lil? You said that Shawn had a message as well. Could this mean that you had something to do with Shawn's murder as well?" He looked at me with fear in his eyes. I couldn't believe that he just asked me that question. I would never do anything to harm my little brother. "Jack listen to me right now, I had nothing to do with Shawn's murder. Do you hear me?" He shook his head, and I could see in his eyes that he believed me. "Something else is going on here I just have to figure it out is all."

We decided to put the file away for the rest of the night and I would work on it tomorrow. I would go talk to people the victims knew and go see their bodies while I talked to the examiner. In the meantime, I was going to spend time with Jack and try and put this out of both our minds for the night. I poured us another shot and said "You know what its time to have this party started." Jack put the music on and jumped up slammed his shot down and started to dance like an idiot. Watching him dancing around like that just to make me laugh I could see why my brother fell for him. They where just alike in almost every way. I couldn't help but have a good time with him even in our darkest days.

The next morning, I got up to find Jack gone. I take my one shot for my hangover and get ready for the day. I had a small list of people that I had to talk to today. 'Hopefully one of them will bring me to a valuable lead.' I thought to myself. I hated that part having to talk to people of the victims. A lot of times even if they're bad people their families want to act like there the pope. Which by there arrest records we can see that they were not anything like their families describe them. But it was just all part of the job and even though I hated that part I knew that it was important. You never know what someone is going to say when they are grieving.

The first victim was Tony Aspen. A middle-aged man with grey hair and blue eyes. He stood about 6 feet tall and 250 pounds which made me wonder how many people it took to hang him on that cross. The first person I wanted to talk to was Tony's girlfriend. The spouse should always be the first one to talk to because they normally give up most of the information. Especially of they had got into a fight the day before. As I pulled up to the house I could see here standing on the porch and see didn't seem all that happy to see me. I could tell she wasn't when I stepped out of my car and started walking towards her when she said "I already talked to the cops." In a very rude way.

"Ma'am I'm detective White and I've just been assigned your boyfriends case. I just have a few more questions for you if you don't mind. I promise I wont take up much of your time." She rolled her eyes as if all I wanted to even be there. 'Let me tell you something honey there are several other places that I rather be there here at your house right now.' I thought to myself. "Fine but like I said to the other cop that showed up here the other day I don't know who wanted him dead other then ever person he has ever came in contact with other then people like him."

"Like him in what way ma'am?" I asked her. Every time she talked I could hear the venom in her voice. "Oh, you know white and straight." "Was he part of any kind of group that you may know of?" I asked her and her reply was simply "Yeah there known as the Nazis." The Nazis? Why wasn't that in the original report. Then I remembered who was on this case before I was. The same idiot that is on it now with me. "Do you by any chance know how to contact any of them." And she just shook her head no. "Just one more question if you don't mind ma'am." She rolled her eyes and just nodded her head. "Was the detective that asked you questions before Todd Jones?" "Yeah, and if you ask me he's not the sharpest tool in the tool shed." Boy she wasn't lying about that for sure. "Thank you for your time ma'am I'll let you know if we have any further questions."

She threw the cigarette that she was smoking into the yard and walked in the house. I got into my car and called Todd. "Hello detective." He said all cheery like his was happy that I was calling him.

"Okay one why is there no mention about the Nazis and two why in the hell do I not have one name from that group." He just sat there on the phone not saying anything. "Listen I'm gonna say this once and only once. You need to find me the group the Nazis ASAP." I hung up the phone. I looked at the list of people I had to interview, and I didn't have anyone else to talk to unless Todd found me the Nazis like I told him to.

A part of me didn't want to contact them and tell them that they all could be in danger. I mean why would anyone want to that, other then it being the right thing to do. I still had to talk to Nelson Patterson, but I didn't have the strength to bring myself to do it. I started driving and got a phone call from Jack. "Hey sis what are you doing?" He said to me it was almost three thirty and I was just mentally drained. "Just gotta go to the office real quick to see if Todd came up with anything regarding a gang." I said to him even though I really didn't want to. "Well call him and find out and get your ass over to my house. I got dinner all ready and a bottle with your name on it."

"What's on the menu tonight?" I asked him knowing that this was his pizza night. I don't know why but for the past five years Wednesday was always pizza. The he said it and I started to laugh at him. "You know that were having pizza if flipping Wednesday. Why are you laughing at me Lil?" "Because you always sound so aggravated when I ask that and I thinks its funny as hell. But I still love you." I could see him rolling his eyes when he said. "I love you to I guess. Now get your ass over here Pizzas getting cold."

I hung up the phone after we said our goodbyes and started to call Todd. When I got to his name I hesitated. I really didn't like to talk to him. And I never called him a detective because to me he would never make it. The guy was dumb as hell when it came to police work. But I had no choice but to work with him because of my boss. She always believed in chances. Me I would have demoted him not promoted him. I pressed the call button and waited for him to answer. "Hello, Lil I don't have anything yet, but I feel as if I'm getting close." I rolled my eyes and said.

"Well, I'm taking the rest of the day off you better have something for me in the morning. And we need to teach you the proper way to question someone cause, I should not have been the one to find out about the Nazis. That information should have been in their file. "Ok detective whatever you think is best. I'll call you tonight if I find anything out." "No just put it on my desk and I see it tomorrow. I just need tonight off." And I hung up the phone.

I knew it wasn't nice to do that, but I really could not stand that man to save my life. I was pulling up to Jack's house where I saw him waiting for me outside. "What are you doing out here? Do you think I forgot where you live?' I asked him. "No, I was staring at the pizza and couldn't take it anymore, so I stepped outside waiting for you. I swear the pizza was telling me to eat it. So get your butt in the house. I'm starving."

We went inside and started to eat. He really was starving because he damn near swallowed three slices in a matter of a few minutes. I went ahead and poured us a shot. After a couple of shots, I was able to eat a couple of slices. We drank damn near the hole bottle, and I crashed on the couch only because I couldn't make it up the stairs, I was so drunk. And Jack went to bed. We weren't prepared for what we woke up to the next morning. It started to feel like a reoccurring nightmare.

Chapter 8

I woke up the next morning in my apartment without any recollection of how I got here. I looked around the apartment and nothing was out of place. I looked down at my hands and I panicked and ran to the bathroom. It happened again I was covered with blood. I went to call Jack to have him come over immediately only to find my phone opened to a text from Todd. There was a list of the Nazis Tony and Nelson was on the top of the list. The next two names on the list where Tim and Bennie. There where about 14 names on the list.

I got out of the text and called Jack. "Lil where in the hell are you I woke up and you where gone. Are you alright?" "No I'm not Jack you need to get over to my apartment right now!" "I'm on my way." And with that he hung up the phone. My phone rang no two minutes after it was Todd. God I didn't have time to deal with him right now but I knew that I had to answer is phone call. I answered the phone but before I could speak Todd spoke. "There's been two more murders. A mister Jackson and Michelson." He said and I remember seeing those names somewhere.

I put him on speaker and looked at the list. They where the next two after Tony and Nelson. What the hell was going on. "Lil are you there?" I didn't say a word I just hung up the phone and put it on the table after I put it on vibrate. I wanted to lock myself in my apartment for the rest of the day. Could I be having a mental break down. What was going on with me. As soon as I sat down with a bottle and two shot glasses and I took a shot. I was sitting in the dark I didn't want Shawn to see me right away. I had those blackout curtains so you would have to turn the lights on to see what I looked like. I didn't bother with a shower.

In a matter of minuets Jack was walking through my door and I was so grateful he didn't live that far. "Why are you sitting in the dark for?" He asked me as he went for the light switch. "NO leave it off at least for a few more minutes. Take a shot with me." I said to him. "Lilly, I have to go to work today. There's no way I can take a shot now." I was getting aggravated with him and I knew that it wasn't his fault. But it didn't stop me from shouting at him. "CALL IN THEN I REALLY NEED YOU HERE!"

He came over to the couch and we both took a shot. He then called into work looked at me and asked "Can I turn the lights on now? What in the hell is going on?" "Take one more shot and then you can turn the lights on. Ok?" I wanted him to be prepared for what he was about to see and even though I haven't seen it yet I knew I was going to look just as bad as the other mornings if not worse. Jack went ahead and took another shot with me and then went for the light switch. "Before you turn that on, I need you to promise that you wont panic."

I knew that would make him worry even more but I didn't need him freaking out either. "Ok ok I wont panic." He said as he turned on the living room lights. When the lights turned on, I could see his face grow pale. I couldn't help myself I just started crying. "What the hell is happening to me Jack? I remember falling asleep on your couch and that's it." He rushed over to me and held me as I cried. "I don't know Lil, but we will figure this out. You have my word."

"Now go take a shower and we will figure out what to do." I was about to do what he asked me to do but then I remembered the two that were found dead. "I didn't tell you everything. Two more people have come up dead. We have linked them all to a gang called the Nazis. What if I'm killing them?" He looked at me and said. "There's no way that you're a killer Lil." We sat there for a few minutes staring at each other and then Jack poured us another shot.

"Then explain to me the blood all over my clothes. Explain to me how four people have been murdered and I find out the same mornings I wake up like this." I did everything I could to hold back the tears that wanted to fall from my eyes. I took another shot with Jack and got up to go shower. Jack grabbed my hand and looked at me with sincerity in his eyes. "Well figure this all out Lilith, I promise you." I squeezed his hand and headed to the bathroom.

When I looked in the mirror I started to cry. How could this be happening to me. I knew in my heart I had killed all four of those men. But why would I that and how. No, I couldn't have done that there's no way. No one kills and doesn't remember. I looked at my bloody hands and realized I was shaking. I got undressed and jumped in the shower washing every bit of my body. Scrubbing it to get every drop of bloody off. No matter how much I scrubbed it still felt as if I missed some.

I must have been in there longer than I thought because Jack knocked on the door. "Hey Lil, you ok in there?" That snapped me out of my thoughts. "Yeah, be out in a minute." I answered and got out of the shower. When I got back into the living room, I could see that he poured another shot. I gave him half of a smile and sat down. I couldn't help but grab that shot and drink it. Without even thinking I poured myself another one and slammed that one down to. Jack just looked at me and shook his head.

"What? I'm kinda going through something right now ya know?" He put his hand on my, like my father used to do. "Do you remember anything? Anything at all?" "There was one time at the first victims' site that um…. Tony, I remember felling déjà vu. Like I had been there before. But that's impossible. Right?" He sat there for a few and then said, "It's possible that you were there before the murder." "No no I felt like I had been there as the murder happened. But how can that be Jack?" I started to cry again and shaking. Jack poured me another shot and I took it. "What don't you want one?" I asked him with a faint smile. "Not until we figure out what we're going to do."

I took another shot and then said "What else is there to do I have to turn myself in." "Are you crazy? What are you supposed to say? Hi, my name is Lilith White and I think I have committed four murders." "Well basically yeah. I mean what else am I supposed to do?" I replied. "Um not turn yourself in for crimes you don't even know you committed for starters. Lets come up with a way to figure out if you did it or not."

"And how do you propose we do that Jack. Someone else might die if I don't turn myself in." "And someone may not. Look I know its not the most ethical way to handle the situation, but we have to be certain before you turn yourself in. Maybe we can lock you in your room and I'll crash on the couch. If you try to leave your room in the middle of the night, we'll know that its you." I thought about his idea for a little bit and agreed to it. "By the way Lil your phone has been going off for about an hour now. I think its that guy Todd you don't like.

"Oh, shit I forgot to call in today." I jumped up to grab my phone when someone knocked on my door. I looked over at Jack and motioned for him to hide the bottle and the glasses. He did and I answered the door. Sure enough Todd was standing there with a file in his hand. "You never came to work or called so captain had me come over to do a check on you. I also thought you would like to get caught up with the case. Were looking at a serial killer now." I moved so that he could come in.

This was perfect I could kind of let Todd know what was going on without my name and see what he thinks. 'He so clueless he might now even be able to keep up with the conversation.' I know I gotta stop being mean I have no idea where this side of me is coming from. I've never been this mean before. But here I am being a bitch in my head. "Please have seat Todd I want to ask you something." I went into the kitchen to grab another shot glass and shook it to Jack to tell him to get the bottle and the shot glasses.

Todd looked at the table as he sat down. I started pouring all three shots. "Oh, none for me I have to get back to the station." I looked at him and put the shot in front of him. "No, you don't. Just call and tell them that you and I are working on the case here. I mean you did bring the file, didn't you?" "Yeah, but I can't lie to the station." Oh my god I have a little good boy on my hands. "Yes, you can now do it or I'm not gonna run this idea by you." I knew that would get to him. He always wanted my approval. Though I could never figure out why. He did exactly what I said to do just like I knew he would.

Jack and I grabbed our shots and Todd reluctantly grabbed his and we all slammed them down. He waited until he drank a couple more and finally asked. "So, what's idea you have." I knew that it was the perfect time because I could tell he was getting buzzed. Jack looked at me in panic. I just put my hand on his knee and started to explain my 'Idea' to Todd. "Well, I was thinking about writing a book about a guy that goes to bed and wakes up covered in blood. Come to find out he's killing in his sleep. What do you think?"

He looked at me puzzled for a minute and then asked. "What will happen to the guy when he finds out?" "That's where you come in. I was hoping that you could tell me what you think he should do." Jack looked over to me and smiled. He finally caught on to what I was doing.

We all took another shot and Todd finally had an answer for me. "I think he should turn his self in. Simply because if they can't find any evidence then he'll be set free."

"Of course, as any good detective knows they always slip up and leave something behind eventually." He then added. Jack spilled a little rum as he was trying to pour it. He looked at me with a panicked face again. I smiled at him as I grabbed my shot, they took theirs as well. Before we knew it the clock had reached nine at night. We called Todd who was three sheets to the wind a cab. After he left, I got the other bottle I had in my freezer. Jack and I where still felt fine I guess because of all the drinking we've done.

"What the hell where you thinking Lil. He could have figured out that you were talking about yourself. Its bad enough we don't know what the hell is going on but now you're putting your self in more danger by even talking about it." I rolled my eyes as I sat back down on the couch. Of course, Jack saw me and gave me a I could kill you look. "Calm down Jack his slow as hell not to mention we got him drunk. The chances that he'll even remember what we talked about are slim to none."

I poured us another shot and we talked the best way to handle the situation at hand. "Well put the camera on your phone on pointing at the door and we'll be able to see what you do if you're sleep walking." Jack said. I just looked at him and said ok. What I was thinking was how the hell could I be sleep walking/killing? It didn't matter I just wanted to get to the end of this any way I could. We had a couple more shots and then set up the camera. Jack tucked me in like I was a kid and locked the door behind him. All I had to do was fall asleep and see what happened in the morning.

Chapter 9

The next morning, I woke up in my bedroom and everything seemed fine. My hands where clean and I felt like I really got some rest. I went to my bedroom door without even thinking about the camera and went to go make coffee. Jack was still asleep on the couch when I passed him. Poor guy sleeping on my couch, and nothing happen. I started making coffee when Jack woke up. I waited till the coffee was made before I left the kitchen. As I was bringing him a cup of coffee he screamed "WHAT THE HELL LILLITH!!!"

I dropped the cup of coffee and the cup shattered. "What why do you have to shout? Look what you've done." I went to go pick up the glass and that's when I saw it. "We need to go to the camera." I said. We ran to the bedroom and I couldn't believe what I was seeing. How could this happen again. I had blood all over me from my elbows up. We went to the nightstand where the phone was and it wasn't there. How could this be? Why is this happening to me? I needed answers and now the only thing that might give them to me some was gone.

I started to flip out not knowing what to do next. Jack started looking through the room and found the camera in the corner on the other side of the room. "Lil calm down I found it." We hooked it up to the television and started to watch it. It started off with Jack leaving the bedroom and locking the door. I fell asleep shortly after that. Then about 30 minutes in I got up and looked straight at the camera with the creepiest smile I've ever seen in my life.

Jack paused the video and stared at the television. "Lil that doesn't even seem like you." I was terrified at this point. How could I seem like a whole other person? Regardless I wanted to see the rest of the video to see what happened last night. I wasn't sure if I could handle it but I knew that no matter what I had to. "Just play the video please I have to see what I did." I asked. "That's the thing Lil the woman in the video is you but its not. I don't know how to explain it but that's not you."

With that I had goosebumps. I knew what he meant. Even though it was me you could tell in my eyes that I wasn't there. We started the video and continued to watch. I put my finger to my lips and said "Shhhh you want to see what I do for fun?" I then looked at my phone and started to scroll. I lifted the camera and then said, "Alright Lilith lets go have some fun with Derek Christopher." I passed the video again and went for the file on the table. Sure, enough the fifth name on the list of the Nazis was Derek Christopher. I looked at Jack and then my phone rang.

I answered the phone. "Hello." It was Rebeca from the station. "Hey detective White we have another murder that seems to be linked to the case you've been working on." I froze 'Please don't say who I think it is please.' I thought to myself. "Hello, are you still there detective?" Yeah, I'm right here. Who was the victim?" "Let me transfer you over to Detective Jones hold on moment please." I wanted for what seemed like forever. Todd finally picked up the phone. "This is Detective Jones how can I help you?"

"Todd it's me Lil I need to ask you who is the new victim?" I looked at Jack on pure terror when Todd said "Derek Christopher. What time are you coming in today I thought we could both go and do the interviews if that's alright with you." I couldn't believe what he just said. The same name that I spoke in the video is dead. The blood that was all over me still must belong to him. I stood there in silence for a moment and then I said "I'm gonna take a personal day. Why don't you go do the interviews?" Without him being able to say another word I hung up the phone.

I was looking at Jack the whole time I was on the phone and he knew something was wrong. "We're gonna need another bottle if we're going to finish that video." I said to him. Luckily for us I had one in the pantry. I grabbed to shot glasses and sad down on the couch next to Jack. "Lil what happened? You look like you saw a ghost." "There was another murder last night. I was that Darek Christopher. He He's dead and I just said his name on the video."

Jack poured us a shot and we sat there for a while on the couch. He let me cry as it really hit me that I not only killed one person but five. How could it be that I turned into the monsters that killed my parents. "Why don't you take another shot and go take a shower." He said to me. I did as he told me to except right before I got up to go take a shower, I took the bottle and took a big swig of the rum.

As I go into the bathroom and started to undress, I stared at myself in the mirror. How could this happen to me? What was happening to me? It was me in the video and my voice. But it didn't seem like me. I looked evil. And if I was the one that did the killing's than I was evil. I thought about this the whole time I was in the shower. And I couldn't for the life of me figure out why this would ever do that to anyone. Was I possessed? Although I didn't believe in possessions, I have to keep an open mind about all the possibilities.

I got out of the shower and got dressed. I went out to thee living room and saw that the video was off. I looked at Jack when I sat down next to him and asked him where the video had went. "Lilith it's not good. But I have news." He poured me a shot and I knew that the news couldn't be good. "Please Jack just tell me what's going on I need to know." I pleaded to him. "Take your shot and I will I swear."

I did what he asked me to do and I sat there looking at him until he stared to talk. "Well from what the video shows you at least killed Darek for sure. I watched his death. But if you did kill the others Darek sang like a canary as to why you would." I just sat there trying to process what he was telling me. "What do you mean he sung like a canary?" I asked. More intrigued that ever. "They killed Shawn Lil." He said that and I just sat there like in a daze.

"H...how do you know that?" I asked even thought I already knew the answer to that question he had just told me that. I didn't want to believe that I killed five people. "Lil you got Darek to tell you that it was his gang. Right before. Well before you slit his throat." I slit someone's throat? How could I do that to someone? And yet I had very little remorse because they where I ones that killed my brother. In fact, the more I thought about it the more I believed that they got what they deserved even if I was the one who did it.

I couldn't think that way. That's not who I am. I care about people that's why I do the job I do to bring some peace to those who lost their loved ones. And yet I'm thinking about these people in such a horrible way. I looked at Jack and told him that I had to turn myself in. "No Lil you cant do that not until we figure out what's going on." "What's there to figure out Jack I'm going out killing people. It's my job to stop anyone who's doing that. I'm even head of this case and the murderer."

Jack wasn't making any since when it came to the matter at hand. How could I not turn myself in. I took an oath to serve and protect and if I'm going around killing people, how am I keeping my word? "Look we don't know if it's even you. Like we know it's you but then again it didn't seem like you." Didn't matter if it was me or not it was my body doing the killings. I had to turn myself in. But as long as Jack was around me, I didn't see him letting me.

I had to figure out a way to get Jack out a way to get Jack out of the house. And I thought that I knew the perfect thing to do. "Why don't you go to your house and grab some clothes. I'll be right here when you get back, I swear." And I wasn't lying to him either. I was going to sit there and thin about what my next move was going to be. He agreed to go and then gave me a hug and said "I'll see you later. Please don't go anywhere." I never knew those where the last words Jack would ever say to me.

Chapter 10

While Jack was gone, I thought about everything that was done as well as everything that Jack and I talked about. I knew that I was right in wanting to turn myself in but on the other hand I knew that Jack was right when he said that it wasn't me. How could I be the one going around killing people? Especially with no recollection of the events. As I was thinking about all of that my phone rang. Something deep inside me told me not to answer but I knew that I had to. Because when I looked at the caller ID I saw that it was the station.

I answered the phone and it was Rebeca but when she said hello she sounded really sad. "Rebeca what is it what's wrong?" There was nothing but silence on the phone for a while. "Bec what is going on this isn't about a case or you would have told me by now." I said and yet she stumbled to say, "It's about Jack." My mind started to race. How long had he been gone? What time was it? What could have happened to him?

"Rebeca, I need you to tell me what is going on with Jack and I need you to tell me know." I said in a calm yet worried voice. "Jack has been." And she stopped right there. I was starting to get made at this point. Why couldn't she just tell me what the hell was going on. "Jack's been in what? What has happened to him?" I found myself screaming into the phone.

"Well Jack has been involved in a murder." She said to me. The next sentence she said to me would crush my very core. "Jack's been killed in the same way that Shawn was. We think they grabbed him when he was leaving his house." I dropped the phone unable to think barely having the capability to breath. This was all my fault.

I made him leave to go get clothes. And I did it for a selfish reason and now he's dead. I ran into the bathroom with the feeling on nausea. I splashed some water on my face and looked in the mirror. What I saw in the mirror wasn't sadness it was anger. I could see the pure anger in my eyes. Without another thought I said out loud 'Let's end this. Let's end them.' I Felt crazy talking to myself but then again, I think I have gone crazy.

I went back into the living room where I had dropped my phone and picked it up. Rebeca had hung up and I was just fine with that. I sat down on the couch and looked at the shot glasses that sat on the table where Jack and I were just using them. I could feel the anger coursing through my veins. Everyone has been taken from me and now I'm all on my own. That's when I heard a voice that said, "You still have me."

I looked around the room and no one was there. I shrugged it off thinking that the voice was in my head and took a shot. I decided to watch the video of me killing that guy Darek. It scared me to see the evil that hid inside of me. But there it was starring at me in the face on my flatscreen television. I could only watch up to the interrogation part. He told me where there hangout was. The barnyard was a dirty biker bar and everyone was a member of the Nazis.

I passed the video as I put the knife up to his neck that would end his life. I poured myself another shot and as I was about to take it, I heard the same voice from before say "The barnyard ha the perfect name for those animals hide a way." Where was that voice coming from? I looked around the room and no one was there. I got up and started to look around the whole apartment. But I couldn't find anyone. I knew that I was hearing a voice and I wasn't going crazy.

As I was walking out of my bedroom, I heard the voice again "Turn around." It said and I froze. I slowly turned around expecting someone to be there and all I saw was my reflection in my tall mirror. I walked over to the mirror very carefully. As if something was going to jump out of it. As I got closer my reflection got bigger. And yet it was only me in the mirror. I must be going crazy if I'm hearing voices. As I went to turn around something in the mirror caught my eye. I quicky turned back around to see me but not doing what I was doing. My reflection was moving on its own.

"What the hell?" slipped out of my mouth in the form of a whisper. "Trippy isn't it." My reflection said to me. I jumped back. I must be going crazy there's no way that this is possible. "Calm down I know what you're thinking and yes you have lost your mind. Well, a part of it anyways." it said. "Wh..what's going on here how is this possible?" I shakenly asked. "It's not you're having a mental breakdown. See when Shawn died something in you snapped and created me. And now that Jack is gone your mind is letting you see the other version of you that you didn't know existed."

Ok so I have lost my mind at least that part was clear. Now to figure out what to do about it. I mean what else could I do but turn myself in and explain to them what happened. I had the video to prove everything that I was saying was true. As I looked at my reflection, I noticed the eyes. They were not my eyes. They where the same eyes we had seen in the video. "You can't turn yourself in yet we must finish what we started." It said to me. "But we didn't start anything you did all of this."

"Tell, me deep down inside what do you want to do to all of them Lilith? You can't possibly want them to stay alive." I wish this voice would just stop talking. No, I didn't want them to live. Why should they after what they did to Shawn and Jack. But I had to trust the courts to do the right thing. Yet there was no prof that they did anything. I would have been told about any evidence that they found. There was only one thing I could do at this point of time. "Lets finish this. But on my terms." I said to it and my reflection smiled an evil crazy smile. "As you wish." And then my refection went back to normal.

I went straight for the bottle and downed as much as I could before I needed a chaser. What the hell was that. I knew one thing was for sure. They did need to all die. And in the video Darek mentioned that they all get together on Friday nights. That was tonight and I was going to take care of them once and for all so they cant hurt anyone ever again. And then I would turn myself in.

I knew that I didn't have it to kill anyone so I was gonna need the voice in my head to do it for me. All I had to do was get drunk go to sleep and it would all be over. But I had things to do before that took place. And I didn't have a whole lot of time. I got the camera and put it on the kitchen table. Along with a note for the police to get after I turned myself in. I knew that they would check my place and I didn't want them to have to look very far.

I then wrote out a detailed letter to the funeral home for them to follow my instructions for Jack's funeral. I also included that he was to be buried next to Shawn. I wrote out a check and sent that out. I also got the other clothes I had worn for the murders. Ok I didn't have that much to do but it still took me a couple of hours to get them done. Once I got everything done, I went back into the living room.

I started to take shots and not really feeling anything. I thought to myself that I should be the one handling this not the psycho voice in my head. But could I do that to people. Well innocent people I could never do that but these guys where anything but innocent. Why shouldn't I do it. I'm about to spend the rest of my life in prison for what. Someone else to do what I need to do? These monsters need to be stopped and I was the one who should take care of them all. But I knew that I didn't have it in me to go through it.

So, I sat down on the couch put on some music and started to take shots. Looking at the shot glass that Jack had used made me realize everything that had happened in such a short amount of time. This had to end no one should be punished for who they love. I felt so alone and nothing could ever fix that. I started to take more shots knowing that by the time I woke up this would all be over.

I fell asleep on the couch well more like I passed out on the couch. I was hopeful that this whole mess would be over again and I would be able to turn myself in. I woke up the next morning in my living room but something felt off to me. Like the weight that was on my shoulders was still there. I checked my phone to see if I had any miss calls. Once I saw that there were none, I checked the news. There was nothing on the news to say anything about anyone that had died. What was going on?

As I was thinking all of these thoughts in my head, I heard the voice that I heard last night. "This you must do on your own." What the hell did that mean I must do it on my own. There's no way that I could do that. "Well then this will never be over cause I cant be the one to end this. You even know how to do it." I did know how to do it. Blow those assholes out of their own building. But did I have it in me to do it.

I thought about Jack and Shawn and I started to get angry. That's when I knew that I could do it. I would have to take the next week planning everything including stealing C4 from the evidence locker. But I knew that I could do it. I sat there on the couch I started to make a list. I got up to get a pen and paper then started to write down everything that needed to be done before and after my plan. I started to shake so I took a shot. Before I knew it, I had the list completed. All there was to do now was to put my plan into play.

Chapter 11

I spent the next week putting together my plan. I had to go to the office and steal C4. So, I decided that the best time to go there would be at night. When I got there Rebecca was still there. But other then that the department was quite. When I got to the evidence room to my surprise there was no one there to check in with. So I quietly went in there and got some of the explosives and put them in the bag that I brought. The bag wouldn't come to any surprise to anyone because I usually have my case files in it.

After I left the room, I went straight for my desk where I saw a few case files and also put them in my bag in order to not be suspected of stealing anything. As I was leaving the department Rebecca called me over to her desk. I thought for sure she knew what I had just done. But I had to act casual. "Yeah, what's up Bec?" I asked her. "I just wanted to tell you how sorry I am to hear about Jack." I just looked at her and left the office. She knew how much I hated pity.

I got to work on the C4 from the books I got from the library. It made me worry about what people can actually access from there. I mean hell I'm learning how to make a bomb in my living room. One that I didn't know for sure if I could actually blow up. Even though I knew that this was the only way to get all of them at the same time. And I knew that I had until tomorrow night to get this bomb ready.

I had already written my letter that I left on Todd's desk. Explaining to him everything that had happened and everything that I had done. I had the camara on the kitchen table for the police to find after my arrest. Tonight, was the night everything would end including the life I had worked so hard to have. I knew deep in my heart that this is what I had to do. Without another thought I finished the bomb and took a shot.

I got to the bar at about Four in the afternoon. I got there early so that I could plant the bomb. I had no idea what I was doing. I've never planted a bomb before. And in a way I have never killed anyone before. How was I going to pull this off? Where was the best place to put the bomb? I decided the best place would be in the women's bathroom. I didn't see any other women in here I was the only one. I then sat at the bar and ordered a drink. I had the bomb to go off with a burner phone that I bought.

I started to look around the bar and they had a in memory for the men that the voice in my head had killed. It pissed me off when I saw it said in memory of our brave fallen brothers. They were anything but brave. Cowards more like it. Killing people for being gay. I couldn't help but think about how many more people they have killed before. Or how many more people that they were planning on killing.

As these thoughts came through my mind, I really didn't feel bad for what was going to happen in the next few hours. I knew that Todd would be here shortly after the fact where I would let him take me in. And then tell him were I left the note on his desk. I made sure to hide it underneath all the files he had. I sat there drinking one after the other trying to wait for everyone to show up. That's when the bartender came up to me and told me they where closing up for a private party.

I left the building and watched as more and more people went into the bar. I knew that this act would probably get me the death sentence but I didn't care. These ass holes took everything from me. And I had nothing to live for anymore. Around eight no one else was showing up and I knew that it was showtime. There was just one thing I wanted to change in my plan, I called Todd.

"Todd, I need you to meet me at the barnyard. I got wind that something is going to happen here." I said to him after he answered the phone. "What's going to happen detective?" He asked me and that caused me to roll my eyes. I hated to many questions and he did one to many. "Look I need you down here now! How far away are you?" He hesitated for a moment then said he was about five minutes away. "Fine meet me over here and don't tell anyone else. They will get all the details later."

I don't know why I called him. Other then in a way this was making it to where I wasn't going to do this by myself. Even if he didn't know what he was about to witness. As soon as he got there he jumped in my car. "Ok what's going on? Why are we here?" he asked. I just looked out at the bar. I pulled out the burner phone out of my jacket pocket and looked at Todd after I got it send to go off after I pressed send. "You might want to get your handcuffs out." I said and pressed the button.

The explosion was bigger then I thought it would be. But boy was it beautiful. It was over it was finally all over. The monsters where gone once again. Shawn and Jack got justice for what happened to them and I was the executioner. I couldn't be happier right now as I watched the building burn to the ground. "WHAT THE HELL JUST HAPPENED!" Todd shouted. I looked over at him and just smiled and said, "It all over now." I got out my handcuffs and handed them to Todd and told him to put them on me.

I stepped out of my car and put my hands behind my back. Todd followed me to my side and started to ask me questions that this time I did not mind answering. "Did you do this?" "Yes" I replied. Why why would you do something like this?" "They killed Shawn and Jack. I only have prof of Shawn but I know in my heart they killed Jack to." "If you knew they where the ones that did it why didn't you let us know?" "Its all on the camara in my apartment." Without another word he handcuffed me and put me in the back of his car.

When we got to the station, I was brought into the examining room where they asked me all the same questions that Todd had asked me. I explained to them everything that had happened. I let them know where the camara was. I told them why I blew up the building and that I knew that I was going away for a very long time. I had no emotion whatsoever about what I had done. I just knew that it was all over and no one else would ever be harmed by those monsters again.

I was brought into booking and then put behind bars. When it came to my attorney, I told her to take the first plea deal that they give us no matter what it was. She argued with me for a bit until she knew that I wasn't going to budge. The plea that they gave us was life in prison without the possibility of parole. I took it with a grain of salt I didn't care that I was going to rot in prison for the rest of my life. I was finally free and my brother and his fiancé got the justice that they deserved.

They got me to the state prison my home for the rest of my life in a very short time. I took my time to read and write about my experience. Which is how your reading this today. But then something horrible happened. I was in the mess hall to go and get my dinner when I heard a voice that shook me to the core. "My beautiful daughter I knew you had it in you. You just needed to be showed the way." It was her my real mother.

Made in the USA
Columbia, SC
07 November 2021